"WITH ONE SPRING HADVOR WAS OUTSIDE THE GRAVE."
Page 135.

Icelandic Fairy Tales.

Icelandic
fairy Tales

Translated and Edited by
MRS. A. W. HALL

With Twenty-two Illustrations
By E. A. MASON

Fredonia Books
Amsterdam, The Netherlands

Icelandic Fairy Tales

Translated and Edited by
Mrs. A. W. Hall

ISBN: 1-4101-0329-3

Fredonia Books
Amsterdam, The Netherlands
http://www.fredoniabooks.com

PREFACE.

FAIRY TALES seem scarcely to require any preface, but in publishing these quaint Norse legends, a few explanatory remarks may not be out of place.

In their original form, many of the stories are somewhat crude and rough for juvenile reading. This it has been the Editor's endeavor to ameliorate by eliminating all objectionable matter, while at the same time preserving the originality and local coloring which most of them possess.

It will be found that though some bear a similarity to the well-known standard fairy tales, which have been the delight of countless children for many generations, yet they all possess an originality peculiarly their own.

It is remarkable too that, whereas in most southern legends it is always the prince who delivers the princess and performs the heroic and valorous deeds, in these tales it is for the most part the young princess or peasant maiden who undergoes all the hardships and trials, and after countless dangers rescues the prince who has fallen under the ban of some wicked witch or giantess.

The story of the five brothers, one of the quaintest, is an exceedingly effective illustration of the old proverb of the bundle of sticks.

A strong moral tone runs more or less through all the tales, exhibiting the higher and better qualities of human nature.

CONTENTS.

ICELANDIC FAIRY TALES.

THE LEGEND OF THE KING'S THREE SONS.

In olden days there once lived a king and a queen; they were wise and good, and their kingdom was known far and near as the happiest and best-governed country in the world. They had three sons—Osric, Edric, and Frithiof,—all handsome and brave and greatly beloved by their parents; but, having no daughter, the king had adopted his little orphan niece Isolde. She grew up with his sons, and was their best-loved playfellow, both the king and queen making no distinction between her and their own children.

As the princess grew older, she also grew fairer, till when she was sixteen years old there was no maiden in the land so beautiful and sweet as Isolde. All three brothers fell in love with her and wanted to marry her, each in turn asking his father for her hand in marriage.

Now the king was greatly puzzled what to do, for he loved his sons all equally well, so at length he decided that the princess should choose for herself, and select the one she liked best. He therefore sent for her, and told her that she was herself to choose as a husband whichever of his sons she liked best.

"It is my duty as well as my pleasure to obey you, dear father," said Isolde; "but when you tell me to choose one of the princes as my husband, you give me a very difficult task, for they are all equally dear to me."

When the king heard these words, he saw that his troubles were by no means at an end, so he thought for a long time how he could best find a way that would satisfy all parties, and at last decided to send all three sons away for a year. At the end of that time they were to return, and whoever had succeeded in bringing back the most precious and valuable thing from his travels should receive the hand of Isolde as his reward.

The three princes were quite willing to accept these terms, and arranged among themselves that at the end of the year they would all meet at their hunting-lodge and thence go together to the king's palace with their gifts; so, bidding farewell to their parents and Isolde, they started off on their different journeys.

Osric, the eldest son, traveled from city to city, and explored various foreign countries, without finding anything precious enough to take home. At last, when he had almost given up all hope, he heard that, not very far from where he then was, there lived a princess who possessed a wonderful telescope, which was so powerful that one could see all over the world with it. No country was too distant, and not only could one see every town, but also every house and tree, and even people and animals inside the houses.

"Surely," thought Osric, "no one could find a more precious or valuable thing than this glass, for nothing is hidden from it." So, having arrived at the castle where the princess dwelt, he told her the object of his journey, and asked whether she would sell him her telescope.

At first the princess said she would not part with it, but when Osric told her how much depended on his taking back so valuable a gift, she consented to let him have it for a very large sum of money.

The prince did not mind this; he only thought the gold well spent, and hastened homewards, full of hope that he would secure the hand of Isolde.

Prince Edric fared much the same as his elder

brother. He also traveled about in distant
countries, seeking in vain for something rare and
precious to bring home. At last, when the year
was nearly at an end, he reached a large and
populous town, and in the inn where he lodged he
met a man who told him that in a cave outside the
town there lived a curious little dwarf called
Völund,* who was famed for his rare skill in all
kinds of metal-work.

"Perhaps," thought the prince, "he might be able
to make me some rare and costly article worthy to
take back." So he went to the dwarf, but when he
told him what he wanted, the dwarf said he was
very sorry, but he had quite given up working in
metals.

"The last thing I made was a shield," he continued, "but that is many years ago now. I made
it for myself, and am unwilling to part with it, for
not only is it almost the finest bit of work I ever
did, but it has also some very special properties."

"And what are these special properties?" asked
the prince.

"Well," replied the dwarf, "it is not only a perfect
safeguard in battle, as no ordinary sword or arrow
can pierce it, but if you sit on it, it will carry you
all over the world, through the air as well as across

* The Norse Vulcan.

the water. But there are some old runes, or ancient letters, carved on the shield, which he who guides it must be able to read. But I will show it you."

So saying, he went to the back of the cave and brought forth a beautiful shield, worked in gold, silver, and copper, the runic letters being all formed of precious stones.

When Edric saw the shield and heard of its wonderful properties, he thought it would not be possible to find anything more rare or valuable. He therefore told the dwarf how much depended on his bringing back so precious a gift, and entreated him to let him purchase it; and he was so importunate and urged him so strongly that, although loth to part with it, when the dwarf heard how much depended on his securing so rare a gift, he agreed to sell it him for a large sum of money. He also taught him how to read the runes, and Edric, thanking him for consenting to part with his shield, started on his homeward journey, filled with hope and confidence that he must win the princess's hand.

Frithiof, the youngest son, was the last to start. He determined to travel through his own country first, so he wandered about from place to place, stopping in this town and that village, and wherever he met a merchant, or hoped to find anything rare or beautiful, he made most searching inquiries. All his efforts, however, proved fruitless. The greater part of the year had already passed, and he was still as far as ever from his goal, and he almost began to fear that no success would crown his efforts.

At length he arrived at a large and populous town, where a big market was being held, and numbers of people from all parts of the world came thronging in, some to buy and some to sell. So he followed the crowd, and then went on from stall to stall, and from one merchant to another, inspecting their wares and chatting and asking for news. But though there were many beautiful and many curious things, nothing specially struck his fancy.

At length, tired and thirsty, he sat down beside a large fruit stall. The merchant, seeing, as he thought, a likely customer, came forward asking if he would not buy something—offering him grapes, peaches, pineapples, and melons in turn.

But Frithiof shook his head ; none of these tempted him, for on the very top shelf he saw a magnificent crimson apple, streaked with green and gold, lying on a bed of soft moss.

"I should like that apple," said the prince, "and do not mind what I pay for it. It is the only thing that I fancy, though all your fruit is splendid."

The merchant smiled. but shook his head.

"You have a quick eye," he said to the prince, "for that apple is indeed the rarest and most valuable thing I have. But it is not for sale. It was given to one of my ancestors, who was a great doctor, by a geni, and has the peculiar power, that if it is placed in the right hand of any one who is sick, no matter how dangerous the illness, they recover at once—aye, even if they are at the point of death—and many a life it has saved."

When the prince heard this, he wished more than ever to possess the apple. He felt he could not possibly find anything that the princess, who was so kindhearted, would value more than the possession of this apple, which would enable her to do good to others. He therefore entreated the merchant to let him buy the apple, and when the man had heard his tale, and all that depended upon his bringing back such a rare and precious gift, he sold the apple to the prince, who, filled with hope, now wended his way homewards.

And so it happened that, as they had arranged, the three brothers arrived at the hunting-lodge, outside the capital, and after they had related their adventures, Osric, the eldest, said, "Now let us hasten to the palace, but before starting I should like to see what the princess is doing."

He thereupon drew forth his telescope and looked

in the direction of the palace, but no sooner had he
done so, than an exclamation of terror escaped his
lips, for there on her couch lay the princess, white
and still as the driven snow, while beside her stood
the king and queen and the chief of the courtiers in
a sorrowful group, sadly awaiting the last breath of
the fair Isolde.

When Osric beheld this grievous sight he was
overwhelmed with grief, and when his brothers
heard what he had seen, they too were overcome
with sorrow. Gladly would each have given all
they possessed to be back in time, at least to bid
her farewell.

Then Prince Edric remembered his magic shield,
which would at once carry them to the king's
palace, and, bringing it forth, the three brothers
seated themselves on it, and the shield rose up in
the air and in a few seconds they had reached the
palace, and hastened up to the princess's chamber,
where they found all the court assembled, sadly
awaiting the end. Then Frithiof remembered his
apple. Now was the time to test its power. Step-
ping softly up to the couch, he bent over the still
white form of the princess and gently placed the
apple in her right hand. Immediately a change
was visible, it seemed as if a fresh stream of life
passed through her body. The color returned to

her lips and cheeks, she opened her eyes, and after a few minutes she was able to sit up and speak.

The general rejoicing at the princess's wonderful and unexpected recovery, and at the happy and opportune return of the three princes, can be better imagined than described.

But as soon as she was quite well, the king, mindful of his promise, called together a great " Thing," or national assembly, at which the brothers were to exhibit the treasures they had brought back, when judgment would be pronounced.

First came the eldest brother Osric, with his telescope. This was handed round for the people to see, while he explained its strange and marvelous properties, stating how by means of this glass he had saved the princess, for he had been able to see how ill she was. He therefore considered that he had earned the right to claim the princess's hand.

Then Edric, the second brother, stepped forth and showed the beautiful shield he had got from the dwarf, and explained its peculiar power. " Of what use would have been my brother's glass," he asked, " without this shield, which carried us hither in time to save her life? I claim, therefore, that it was really due to the power of my shield that the princess is not dead, and that I ought therefore to possess her hand in marriage."

And now it was Frithiof's turn to come forward with the apple. He said, "I fear that neither the telescope which first showed us that the princess was ill, nor the shield which so quickly brought us hither, would have sufficed to restore the Princess Isolde to life and health, had it not been for the magic power of my apple. For what good could our mere presence have done her? Our seeing her thus and unable to help her, would only have added to our grief and pain. It is due to my apple that the princess has been restored to us, and I therefore think my claim to her hand is the greatest."

Then there arose much questioning and reasoning in the "Thing" as to which of the three articles were of the greatest value, but as they could come to no satisfactory agreement, the judges declared that all three articles were of equal value, for they had all equally contributed to restore the princess to life and health, for if one had been missing, the other two would have been valueless. So judgment was pronounced that, all three gifts being equally valuable, neither of the brothers could claim the princess's hand.

Then the king happily hit upon the idea of allowing his sons to shoot for the prize, and whoever was adjudged the best shot should wed the princess.

So a target was set up, and Osric, armed with bow and arrow, stepped forth first.

Taking careful aim, he drew his bow, and the arrow sped forth, but it fell some distance short of the mark.

Then Edric stepped forth. He too took careful aim, and his arrow fell nearer the mark.

And now it was Frithiof's turn. He too took a very careful aim, and all the people said his arrow went beyond the mark, and that he was the best shot, but when they came to look for it, behold, it could nowhere be found. In vain search was made in all directions, no sign of the arrow could be found. The king therefore decided that Edric had won the princess's hand. The wedding forthwith took place amid great splendor and rejoicing, and the princess and her husband then went to her own country, where they reigned long and happily. The eldest brother, Osric, greatly vexed that he had not been successful, started off on a long journey, and nothing more was heard of him. So only the youngest brother was left at home. But he was not at all satisfied with the way matters had turned out, for he had always been considered by far the best shot. He therefore searched every day in the field where the trial had taken place, looking for his arrow. At length, after many days, he found it lodged in an oak tree, far beyond the mark. He brought witnesses to attest the truth of this, and though there could be no question that his arrow had gone the furthest, the king said it was now too late to go into the matter, for the princess was married and gone away.

Then Frithiof grew very restless. He thought he had been unfairly treated, and at length decided to go away, so he packed up his belongings, and, bidding his parents farewell, started off in search of adventures.

After passing along the wide plains that surrounded the capital, he climbed a high range of mountains, and from thence descended into a great forest. Here he wandered about for several days, but whichever way he turned, he could see nothing but trees all around him. The small store of food he had taken with him when he started was exhausted, and tired, hungry, and footsore, he sat down to rest on a large flat gray stone, unable to proceed any further. He thought the end of his days had surely come, when suddenly he heard the noise of horses' feet, and looking up he saw ten men mounted on horseback coming rapidly towards him. They were all richly dressed and well armed, the last one leading a finely caparisoned palfrey.

When they came to the prince, the leader dismounted, and, bowing low before him, begged him to honor them by mounting the steed they had brought with them.

Frithiof gratefully accepted this offer, and, mounting the horse, the party turned back the way they had come, riding rapidly on till they arrived at a large town. Before entering the gates they dismounted, the prince alone remaining on horseback, and then led the prince in state to the palace.

Now, it happened that a most beautiful young queen reigned over this province. She had been left an orphan at an early age, her father entrusting his chief ministers with the care and responsibility of looking after her and finding her a worthy husband. Queen Hildegard received the prince with much friendliness. She told him that her fairy godmother had bestowed on her the gift of seeing, whenever she wished, what happened in other countries.

"A wandering minstrel came here and told us of the wonderful journeys you and your brothers had made, and also of your sorrow at your failure in the shooting competition for the Princess Isolde's hand, though you were the best shot of the three. Then a great wish seized me to try and make you happy, so I followed your wanderings after you left your father's palace, and when I saw you, sad and tired, resting on the great stone in my forest, I sent forth some of my knights to meet you and bring you back, and now, with the consent of my ministers, I invite you to remain here as my husband. You shall rule over my kingdom, and I will try, as far as lies in my power, to make you forget all the trouble and anxiety you have gone through."

Frithiof was charmed with the beauty and kindness of the maiden, and gladly consented to share her throne, and very happy days followed for both of them. The wedding was on the most magnificent scale, and after they were married, Frithiof, according to the custom of the country, took the reins of government in his hands, amid the general rejoicing of the people.

And now we must return to the old king. Soon after his youngest son had gone away the queen died, and the king, well advanced in years, felt very lonely and dull. One day, while seated beside the great open hearth, in the big audience hall, a pedler woman entered and displayed her wares before him. She told him her name was Brunhilde—she had evidently traveled much—and amused the king with tales of where she had been and what she had seen.

When she was going away, the king told her she might come again, which she did, day after day, till the king got so interested in her talk, that he never was happy unless Brunhilde was with him, and at length asked her to marry him and be his queen.

In vain the chief ministers and courtiers dissuaded him from taking this step. The king was determined, and the wedding took place.

No sooner had Brunhilde gained her object, than she showed that she meant to be a real queen, not merely one in name. She always sat beside the king in council, and interfered in all State matters. He would do nothing without consulting her, and no matter how wrong or unfair it might be, he always did whatever she wished.

One day she said to him, " It seems very strange to me, that you have never made any attempt to recall your son, who went away. Why, only the other day we heard that he had become king of a neighboring country. You may depend upon it that, as soon as he has got a sufficiently large army, he will come back and attack you here, in order to revenge himself for the fancied wrong he imagines was done him, in the trial of skill for the princess's hand. Now, take my advice, call out your army, attack him first, and so ward off the danger that threatens your country."

At first the king would not listen to what the queen said, and declared she was only frightening herself for nothing. But Brunhilde brought forward fresh arguments each day, till at length the king thought she must be right, and asked her what he had better do, so that the prince should not suspect anything.

"You must first send messengers to him with presents," said the queen, "and invite him to come and see you, so that you may arrange with him about his succession to the throne after your death, and also to strengthen the friendship and neighborly relations between your two countries. After that we will consult further."

The king thought her advice very good, and at once sent messengers laden with presents to his son.

When they arrived at Prince Frithiof's court, they told the young king how anxious his father was to see him, and hoped he would make no long tarrying in coming to visit him.

Frithiof, greatly pleased with the handsome gifts his father had sent him, at once agreed to go, and hastened to make all preparations for his journey. But when Queen Hildegard heard of it she became very anxious, and entreated her husband not to leave her.

"I feel that some danger threatens you, and that you may even lose your life," she said.

But Frithiof laughed at her fears. "Surely you do not think my father would entreat me to come to him if he meant to deal wrongly with me ?   No, no, dear wife; set your heart at rest, and have no fears.   I will make but a short stay ; " and so saying he bade her a fond farewell and started off with the messengers, arriving after a short journey at his father's court.

But instead of the warm greeting promised him, to his surprise the king received him but coldly, and began to reproach him for being so undutiful as to go away.

"It was most unfilial behavior," broke in the queen, "and caused such grief to your father that he was nearly at death's door ; and had anything happened to him, your life would have been forfeited, according to the laws of the land.   As, however, you have given yourself up willingly, and have come here when he sent for you, he will not condemn you to death, but he gives you three tasks to perform, which you must accomplish within the year."

It was in vain that Frithiof declared he never meant to vex his father.   The queen would not let the old king speak, and said the only way Frithiof could save his life was to carry out the tasks his father had set him, which were as follows :—

"First, you must bring back a tent large enough to seat a hundred knights, and yet so fine and thin that you can cover it with one hand ; secondly, you must bring me some of the famous water which cures all sicknesses; and, thirdly, you must show me a man who is utterly unlike any other man in the whole world."

"And in what direction must I go to find these rarities?" asked Frithiof.

"Nay, that is your affair," said the king; when Brunhilde, taking his arm, led him away into his own chamber; and Frithiof, without other farewell, sorrowfully returned to his own kingdom.

On his arrival, Queen Hildegard hastened down to meet him, and seeing him looking sad and silent, asked him anxiously how he had fared at his father's court.

At first Frithiof, not liking to frighten her, tried to put her off, and made light of the scant courtesy shown him; but Hildegard, kneeling down beside him, and taking his hand in hers, entreated him to conceal nothing from her.

"I know you have had some difficult tasks given you, which will not be easy to perform. But do not lose heart, dear husband. Tell me all, and then we will see if some way cannot be found to carry them out. A thing bravely faced is half accomplished, and it is not at all impossible that with my kind god-mother's help I may be able to aid you. Tell me, therefore, what makes you so anxious."

Then Frithiof, taking heart, told Hildegard of the difficult tasks that the queen had given him to do. "And if I fail to accomplish them within the year I must forfeit my life," he concluded.

"This is surely your stepmother's doing," said Hildegard. "She is a jealous and, I fear also, a wicked woman. Let us hope she is not planning any further mischief against you. She evidently thought these tasks she gave you would be more than you could accomplish; but, fortunately, I can help you in some of them. The tent your father wants I happen to have; it was given me by my godmother, so that difficulty is disposed of. Then the magic water which you are to bring is not far from here. Nevertheless it is not easy to get, for it is in a deep well, inside a dark cave, which is guarded by seven lions and three huge snakes. Several persons have tried to get in and fetch some of the water, but no one has ever yet come back alive. I might give you some poison to kill these monsters, but, unfortunately, the water loses all its healing power if it is taken after the animals are dead. But I think I may nevertheless be able to help you get it."

Queen Hildegard then sent for her cowherd, and he and his assistants drove seven oxen and three great boars to the mouth of the cave. Here the animals were killed. and the carcasses thrown down before the lions and snakes. Then, while the monsters were gorging themselves with the carcasses of the dead animals, the queen told Frithiof to lower her quickly down the well. She had provided herself with a large crystal jar; this she immediately filled with the water, and when Frithiof drew her up again, so exactly had she timed it, that they both reached the mouth of the cave just as the lions and snakes were finishing the last morsels of their meal. Thus the second task was safely accomplished, and Frithiof and Hildegard hastened back to the palace.

"The two first tasks are happily ended," said Hildegard; "but the third and most difficult one still remains to be done, and this you must carry out by yourself. All I can do is to tell you how best to set to work about it. You must know that I have a half-brother, called Randur. He lives on an island not very far from here. He is nine feet high, has one big eye in the middle of his forehead, and a black beard thirty yards long, and as hard and stiff as pigs' bristles. He also has a dog's snout instead of a mouth and nose and a pair of green cat's eyes. In truth, it would be impossible to find another creature like him. When he wants to go from one place to another, he swings himself along by means of a great pole fifty yards long, and in this way he almost seems to fly through the air like a bird. The island on which he lives forms about one-third of my father's kingdom, and my brother thought he ought to have had a larger share. Then, also, my father had a wonderful ring which my brother wished to keep, but this also fell to my share, and since then my brother has shut himself up in his island. Now, however, I will write to him, enclosing the ring he always coveted. Perhaps that may dispose him to be more friendly to us, and we may get him to go to the king's court; for I know no one else who could so well fulfil the third task given you. Now, therefore, you must go to him accompanied by a large following of knights and squires, for that will please him. When you come near his castle, take off your crown, and approach his throne bareheaded. He will then stretch forth his hand, and you must bend your knee and kiss it, and then hand him my letter and the ring. If after reading it he tells you to rise and seat yourself beside him, we may hope that he will aid us. And now, good luck attend you!"

Frithiof followed the queen's instructions exactly. When he arrived at the three-eyed king's palace, both he and his attendants were greatly startled at the frightful ugliness of the three-eyed monarch; but quickly recovering himself, Frithiof handed him Hildegard's letter and the ring. When the giant saw the ring he seemed greatly pleased, and said—

"I suppose my sister wants my help in some important matter, that she sends me so valuable a present?"

He then bade Frithiof sit down beside him, and, having read his sister's letter, he said he was quite ready to help and carry out her wishes.

He then stretched out his hand, grasped the long pole that always rested near him, and in an instant he had swung himself out of sight.

The king feared at first that Randur had gone away altogether and left them, but a loud shout told them he had only gone in advance. And thus they went on, the giant waiting for them every now and then, and when they reached him scolding them well for being so slow and dilatory; in this way they at last arrived at the queen's palace, and Randur at once asked Hildegard what it was she wanted him to do.

The queen then told him what Frithiof's father had required of her husband, and begged her brother to accompany Frithiof back to his father's court. Randur, greatly pleased at having at last got the ring he so much coveted, declared himself quite ready to do as she desired. So they started off at once for the old king's palace, which they reached without any further adventures.

Frithiof announced his arrival to his father; but though he informed him that he had obtained the three things required of him a year ago, he carefully kept Randur in safe hiding till his presence should be required, and asked that a "Thing" might be called together, in order that he might show the people how he had succeeded in carrying out the tasks assigned him.

So the old king issued a proclamation all through the land, and on the appointed day so great was the interest and curiosity of every one, from the king and his courtiers down to the very poorest laborer and herdboy, that there was hardly standing-room in all the great "Thing" valley.

Queen Brunhilde was furious at the thought that Frithiof should have been successful, but she still hoped that, when the things were brought to light, it would be found that he had failed in something.

The tent was produced first. When it was fairly set up, it was so large and roomy that a hundred knights and squires easily found room inside, yet it was so finely wrought, that when closed any one could cover it with their hand. So all the people declared Prince Frithiof had fully acquitted himself of his first task.

Then the prince brought forth the crystal jar with

the healing water, and handed it to his father. Queen Brunhilde, who was getting quite yellow with anger, insisted upon tasting it to see whether it was the right water and taken at the right time, so as not to lose its healing qualities. But as she was quite well, no sooner had she tasted the healing water, than she felt very ill, and had to take a second taste ere she was well again. So the second task was pronounced to have also been successfully accomplished.

"Now," said the king, "there only remains the third and last task, and that was the most difficult one. See that you have not failed in that."

Then Frithiof sent for the three-eyed giant, whom he had kept in safe hiding till now.

When Randur appeared before the "Thing" springing into their midst by means of his long pole, every one, but especially the old king, started back in fear; they could not imagine how he had got there, and thought he must have flown down from the skies. Never before had they seen so hideous a creature. But, not taking any notice of the crowd, Randur walked up to the queen, and placing the point of his long pole against her chest, he raised her up in the air, and then hurled her to the ground, when she fell down dead, and was immediately transformed into the hideous old giantess she really was.

Having accomplished this, Randur made his way out of the "Thing," and returned to his island.

Frithiof devoted all his efforts to restore and nurse the old king, who, through anxiety and fright, had nearly been at death's door. But a few drops of the healing water sprinkled over him quickly re-

"WHEN RANDUR APPEARED BEFORE THE 'THING,'"

stored him, and being freed by the queen's death from all her wicked enchantments, he speedily recovered his former good sense, and found that all the faults he had thought his son guilty of, were only the inventions of wicked Queen Brunhilde.

He therefore called Frithiof to his bedside, and

begged him to forgive him all the injury he had tried to do him.

"I am only anxious now to make up to you, my dear son, for all you have suffered, and beg you never to leave me again. I will gladly hand over the kingdom to you, and live beside you in peace and quiet for the rest of my days."

So Frithiof was reconciled to his father, and at once sent messengers to Hildegard, telling her what had happened, and begging her to hasten to him. Queen Hildegard, when she received her husband's message, decided to give up her small kingdom to her brother, as a reward for all he had done for them; and then, accompanied by some of her husband's ablest courtiers and friends, she rejoined Frithiof, and the old king, happy at having his son again, lived to a good old age, surrounded by his grandchildren and great-grandchildren.

HELGA.

An old man and his wife once lived in a cottage beside the sea, far away from any other habitations. They had three daughters; the eldest was called Fredegond, the second Olga, and the youngest Helga.

Now, although the parents were not rich, owning only a few acres of land, which they tilled themselves, Fredegond and Olga were treated as if they were princesses. They never did any work, but sat all day amusing themselves and decking themselves in any finery their father brought them home from the neighboring town, whilst Helga, who was far more beautiful and clever than either of her sisters, was always kept in the background. She never shared in any pleasures that her elder sisters often enjoyed; no presents were ever brought home for her; but all day long, from early morning till late at night, poor Helga had to work and toil for the whole family, receiving nothing but sour looks, often accompanied by blows, from the elder sisters.

Now, it happened one day that the fire on their hearth had been allowed to go out. Helga was busy working in the fields, and as they had to send a long way to fetch fresh fire, the old man told Fredegond she must go for it.

At first Fredegond grumbled, for she was trying to dress her hair in a new way ; but then she thought a walk through the woods might be pleasant, so she started.

After she had gone some little distance, she came to a hillock, and heard a deep voice saying, "Would you rather have me with you or against you ?"

Fredegond, thinking it was some laborer or wood-cutter, said she did not care in the least, and that it was very impertinent of him to address her, and went on to the cave whence they fetched their fire.

When she got there, to her great surprise she saw a big caldron, filled with meat, boiling on the fire, and beside it stood a pan, filled with dough, wait-ing to be made into cakes, but not a creature in sight.

Fredegond, being very hungry after her long walk, stirred up the fire beneath the caldron, to make the meat boil quickly, and then began baking some cakes. But although she made one specially nice for herself, she let all the others burn, so that they were quite uneatable. Then as soon as the meat was cooked she took a bowl from a shelf, filled it with all the best bits, and sat down and made a good meal, finishing up with the cake.

Just as she had finished, a big black dog ran up to her, and began wagging his tail and begging for some food. But Fredegond angrily gave him a slap, and chased him away. Then the dog grew angry, and, jumping upon her, bit one of her hands.

Screaming with fright and pain, Fredegond jumped up, and, in her hurry to get away, forgot all about the fire she was to bring, and ran home to tell her parents what had happened.

They were very sorry, both for her sore hand, which they bathed and bandaged, and the lack of the fire. It was really very unfortunate, for that cave was the nearest place where they could procure some fire, as it was generally used by charcoal-burners. So, though very unwilling to send Olga, who was their pet and favorite, she had to go, for they all feared that if Helga were sent, she might run away and never come back again. And then there would be no one on whom to vent their bad tempers, or to do the work of the whole household —for did she not wait on father and mother and both her sisters? So it was decided that Olga should go.

But, alas! Olga fared even worse than her sister.

She was so spoilt, that she thought she ought always to have the best of everything. So, when she reached the cave, she too helped herself to all the best bits of meat, and, making a nice cake for herself, threw the rest of the dough on the fire.

Then when the dog came up to her and wagged his tail and sat up and begged for some food, Olga took up some of the boiling broth and threw it on him. This made the dog so angry that he jumped up and bit off the point of her nose; and Olga ran home crying and screaming, with only half a nose and no fire.

This time the parents were quite beside themselves with anger, and decided that Helga must go and fetch the fire. If she succeeded, well and good; and if not, why, the dog might eat her, for all they cared. It would be a good riddance.

So, taking up the big fire-shovel, Helga went on her way to the cave. As she passed the hillock, she too heard a voice, saying, "Would you rather I was with you than against you?"

To this question she answered, "A well-known proverb says, ' There is nothing so bad that it is not better to have it on your side than against you;' so, as I do not know who you are who ask me this question, I would rather that you were with me than against me."

And hearing nothing further and seeing no one, Helga continued her way till she reached the cave. Here she found everything the same as her sisters had done. The caldron was on the fire, and the dough was ready for baking, but, instead of thinking only of herself, Helga looked after the meat, and saw that it was nicely cooked; then, with great care, she made up the dough into cakes, and never thought of taking anything for herself, although she was very hungry, for she had had nothing for her breakfast but some hard, dry crusts, and a glass of cold water. Neither would she now help herself to any of the fire without asking leave from the owner of the cave.

Feeling very tired after her long walk, Helga sat down on a bench to rest. But she had hardly done so, when she heard a loud rumbling noise; the ground began to tremble; and Helga, fearful that the cave might fall in, rose hastily from her seat. But as she turned to run out, she saw a big, three-headed giant standing at the entrance of the cave, followed by a large black dog.

Helga was terribly frightened; but being fond of animals, she held out her hand and patted the dog, and she quite regained courage when the giant, in a kind voice, said, "You have done the work well, which you found waiting here. It is only right, therefore, that you should get your share. Sit down, therefore, on that bench, and share my dinner; afterwards you can take home some of the fire you have come for."

The giant then got a bowl from the shelf and

"SHE SAW A BIG THREE-HEADED GIANT."

helped Helga to some broth out of the big caldron, carefully giving her the tenderest bits of meat. As he did so, the ground again began to shake and tremble, and fearful noises, like claps of thunder, frightened Helga greatly.

But the giant in a gentle voice bade her sit down beside him, and she finished her broth.

Then the giant got up and gave her one of the cakes she had baked ; but no sooner had she finished it, than the ground again began to shake and tremble, the thunder pealed, and flash after flash of lightning lit up the inside of the cave. Helga got so terrified that she ran up to the giant for protection, and as she clung to his arm the noises ceased, and as the darkness passed away Helga saw that the giant had disappeared, and that she was holding on to the arm of a handsome young prince.

"Nay, do not be frightened," he said ; "I can never thank you enough, dear Helga, for you have rescued me from the horrible enchantment the wicked fairy Gondomar pronounced on me at my birth. I am Torquil, the son of King Osbert, who reigns in the neighboring island ; but because my father refused to marry Gondomar, and chose my mother instead, the wicked fairy condemned me to go through life a three-headed monster, until some young girl should, despite my frightful appearance, place full trust and confidence in me."

As Prince Torquil said these words, he seated himself beside Helga on a stone, thickly covered with soft green moss. Then Helga told him her history, and why she came to the cave, and also the fate of her sisters who had gone to the cave on the same errand, adding that she must hasten back with the fire, else her father and mother would scold and beat her.

"You shall not be ill treated any more," replied Torquil; and he went to the back of the cave, and presently returned, carrying a casket and a small bundle in his hands.

"See, this casket contains gold, and pearls, and precious stones," he said. "You can give some of these to your sisters; but this," and he placed the bundle on a stool, "you must wear under your own dress, when you get home, and be very careful that no one sees it."

So saying, he undid the bundle, and unfolded a beautiful dress of cloth of gold, all worked with silver and precious stones.

Helga could not repress a cry of admiration when she saw the lovely gown, and warmly thanked the prince for all his beautiful gifts.

Torquil then filled her fire-shovel with burning coals, and carried it for her some part of the way home; but ere they came in sight of the cottage he stopped, and, taking her hand, placed a heavy gold ring on her finger.

"Keep this ring, dear Helga," he said, "and let no one take it from you. It will not be long ere I come to claim my bride, but I must first return to my parents and tell them the joyful news that the wicked charm is broken at last." With these words he took a loving farewell of Helga, and started her on her homeward journey.

When she reached the cottage, and her parents saw that she had succeeded in bringing back the fire, Helga, for once in her life, received a kind word of welcome ; but when she showed them the casket and was about to give her sisters some of the jewels, they seized upon it, and dividing the contents among themselves, returned Helga the empty casket. They might also have taken away her beautiful dress, but, after Torquil left her, she had taken the precaution to slip it on under her old gown, so no one knew anything about it.

And thus some days passed on. Matters relapsed into their former way. Fredegond and Olga did nothing all day but deck themselves with the jewels out of the casket, quarreling and fighting over them, and Helga, as before, had to do the work for the whole family, when one day the mother, who had been to the higher meadow for some herbs she wanted, came back and said that she had seen a beautiful big ship lying at anchor on the shore below their cottage.

The old man hastened down to the strand to find

out who the owner of the fine vessel might be, and seeing a boat pulling off from it, he waited till the stranger, who was a handsome young man, had landed, and then entered into conversation with him. But though he plied him with many questions, he could not find out his name.

Then the young man in his turn began to question him, and asked him how many children he had.

" Only two daughters," replied the old man, " and such good and beautiful girls they are too," he added.

" I should much like to see them," said the stranger.

The old man, greatly delighted, led the way back to his cottage, where his two eldest daughters had hurried on their best frocks and decked themselves with all the jewels out of Helga's casket.

The stranger expressed himself as being very pleased with the girls.

" But," he asked, " why has one of your daughters got her hand tied up with a cloth, and the other one a handkerchief fastened across her nose ? "

At first the father said they had met with an accident, and slipped down the cliffs ; but when the stranger pressed for further particulars, the story of the dogs and the cave had to be told.

" But surely you have another daughter ? " said

the stranger; "one who, I know, is always kind to all animals."

At first the old man and his wife both declared they only had those two daughters; but when the stranger kept on urging him, he at last admitted that he had another girl. "But she is so ugly, lazy, and wicked," he added, "that she is more like some wild animal than a human being."

But the stranger said he did not mind that at all, and that he must see her. So the old man was obliged at last to call Helga.

The poor girl came out from the kitchen dressed just as she was, in her shabby old dress, when the young man went up to her; and as he took her hand the ragged old gown slipped from her shoulders, and there, to the astonishment and rage of her sisters, stood Helga, arrayed in the beautiful garment the prince had given her.

Prince Torquil rated the old man and the two wicked sisters soundly for all their unkindness to Helga. He also made the sisters give up all the jewels they had taken from her. But Helga begged that they might be allowed to keep a few; and the prince consenting, she gave each of them two chains, two brooches, two bracelets, and two pairs of ear-rings. Then Torquil led Helga down to the shore and took her on board his beautiful ship, where his

sister gave her a kindly welcome; and when they
reached his own country, King Osbert and his queen
prepared a great wedding-feast, and Torquil and
Helga were married, and lived long and happily together.

THORSTEIN.

CHAPTER I.

HOW THORSTEIN LOST HIS KINGDOM.

THERE once reigned a king and queen, a long, long time ago, who had an only child, a son called Thorstein.

The lad was brave, strong, and handsome, and was greatly beloved by every one on account of his kind-heartedness and open-handed generosity.

But as years passed and he attained to man's estate, his indiscriminating kindness was often taken advantage of. His father and mother tried to check him, pointing out that heedless generosity often did more harm than good; but Thorstein could not be brought to believe that kindness could ever be wrong or do harm, and continued to give to every one who asked him, as long as he had anything he could part with.

At length the king and queen died. On their death-bed they again endeavored to impress upon their son that a good and wise king must not only reign with kindness, but also with justice; but though Thorstein, who loved his parents dearly, and was terribly grieved at the idea of losing them, promised he would do his best and bear their wise counsel in mind, no sooner were the burial ceremonies concluded and he was crowned king, than all his good resolves to be firm and discriminating were scattered to the winds.

He kept open house for all who chose to come, gave gifts to all who asked, so that all the riches and treasure his wise father had so carefully collected began very speedily to disappear, without any one being really the better or happier for them.

So quickly indeed did all he had inherited vanish, that ere many months had passed he had nothing left but the kingdom itself; and then realizing the truth, that a penniless king has but small authority or power, he decided to part with his throne, and thus have some money wherewith to make a fresh start in life.

There was no difficulty in finding a purchaser, and Thorstein, in exchange for a horse and a sack filled with gold and silver, parted with his inheritance.

But when he had once sold his kingdom, his so-called friends, who had been so numerous before, now speedily began to drop off, and as the sack got emptier, so did his companions grow fewer in number.

"There will soon be nothing more to be got out of him," they said. "A fool and his money is soon parted." So they gradually deserted him.

Then, when it was too late, Thorstein began to realize the sad plight he had brought himself to, and determined to quit the country, and leave his false friends behind him. He therefore put together the few things he had left, placed them on the horse he had bought, and mounting his own fine chestnut, which he could never bring himself to part with, he started off on his travels.

For a long time Thorstein wandered on over desolate moors and through dark somber forests, not knowing or caring where he went or what became of him. He had no friends, not a single creature to care for, or who loved him, so he allowed the horses to roam where they listed, letting them graze whenever they came to any fresh grass, but beyond this never resting or pausing anywhere.

Once, when they had stopped to graze near a tiny stream on the banks of which the grass looked specially fresh, he got off his horse, and throwing himself down on the ground almost made up his mind to go no further. Why not rest there till death overtook him? But even as this thought flashed through him, he raised his eyes towards the west, where the sun was just setting in a bed of crimson and gold, flushing all the distant peaks of the great snow-capped mountains with magic rainbow hues.

Whilst still lost in wondering admiration at the gorgeous spectacle, the rosy clouds suddenly parted, and a star of exquisite brilliancy shot down a ray of light that seemed to touch Thorstein's face, and he heard a voice saying: " Fear not, Thorstein, but go forth on thy travels with a brave heart. Learn from the mistakes of thy youth, that indiscriminate open-handedness is neither just nor kind, but only does harm, and that a true sovereign must also be a father to his people."

And even as the voice died away, the rosy light gradually faded from sky and mountain, and the pale golden moon rose and shed its soft silvery radiance over earth and sky.

Thorstein started to his feet. He felt the warm blood coursing quickly through his veins; and whistling to his horses, who came obedient to his call, he mounted his noble chestnut with a light heart, fully determined to seek his fortune.

CHAPTER II.

HIS ARRIVAL AT THE GIANT'S CASTLE.

FOR some time he followed the rough track across the open plain, but presently he arrived at a small farm. Knocking at the door, he asked the old man who opened it if he might rest the night there.

" Oh yes," replied the man ; " if you don't mind taking things as you find them, you are very welcome."

Thorstein thanked him kindly, and after stabling his horses in the shed at the back, threw himself down on the rushes that were lying in one corner of the room, the farm servants occupying the opposite corner, and the old man sleeping in a third corner, the remaining one being filled by the huge stove.

Thorstein, tired out with his long day's journey, slept soundly all night, but when he woke next morning he was surprised to find the farmer and his men had already gone out.

Fearing lest some treachery might be meditated, he sprang up from his bed and rushed out of the house.

There, to his surprise, he saw the farmer and all his men busily at work with their pitchforks, digging and raking up the earth from a large tumulus, or grave, at some little distance from the farm.

Thorstein hurried up to the farmer, and asked him what he was doing, and why he was disturbing the grave.

"I have very good reason for doing so," replied the man; "the man who lies buried there owes me two hundred dollars!"

"But," said Thorstein, "no amount of digging will give you back the money he owed you! On the contrary, you are losing your own time as well as that of your men, and you will probably, in addition, get fined for disturbing the grave."

But the farmer was obstinate. He said he did not care. Only he was quite determined that the dead man should not rest peacefully in his grave, while he owed him all that money, and that he and his men would continue to dig and stir up the ground day after day.

Then Thorstein asked him if he would be satisfied and let the man rest in his grave if some one else paid the dead man's debt.

"Oh yes!" answered the farmer; "but I don't see where that man is likely to come from, as he had no sons."

Then Thorstein drew forth his purse, which contained the last of his money, and gave it to the farmer in payment of the debt. The farmer thanked him warmly, and promised not to disturb the **grave** **any** more.

So Thorstein bade his host farewell; but ere **he** left he asked him which road he should take, **so as** to reach a populous neighborhood, where he might chance to get some work to do.

"You must continue along this same road," replied the farmer, "until you come to four cross-roads. Then don't take the road that goes east, but **take** the one that goes west."

Thorstein thanked him, and rode away. After some time he arrived at the cross-roads, and took the road to the west, as the farmer had advised him. But he had not gone very far when he thought he would rather like to know why the man had said he should not go the other way.

"Perhaps there are giants or some other dangers one may meet," thought Thorstein; so he promptly turned back till he arrived at the cross-roads, when he proceeded along the road leading east.

For some time he saw nothing new or strange. The road wound among many small fields and brush-wood, with here and there some groups of tall, dark pine-trees; but after passing through a narrow defile, he suddenly came to a large, deep valley, in the center of which rose a fine big house, standing quite by itself on a steep, rocky mound. At first he could see no way of getting up to it, but presently he noticed a narrow path, almost hidden by trees and thicket; so, fastening his horses to a stake, he made his way up to the house.

As he approached he saw the door was wide open and no one anywhere about. Thorstein therefore went in and came into a big hall, in which stood two huge beds, one on each side, covered with rich silken hangings, while down the middle ran a table, ready laid with two plates, two knives and forks, two great goblets of rarely chased silver, and two large golden flagons of wine. But no one was visible here either.

After waiting a short time, to see if the owners would appear, Thorstein went down the hill again to look after his horses, for he thought he might as well stay the night in the house, even if there were a little danger in so doing. So he lifted the saddles off the horses, tethered them with sufficient length of rope that they could both graze and lie down comfortably, and then took all he needed out of his saddlebags, with his sword, which, after his favorite chestnut, was his most precious possession. Then, giving a last look to the horses to see they were all right, he returned to the house, and going to the kitchen, he brought thence some bread and the meat which was roasting before the fire.

Cutting this up carefully, he placed a good portion in each plate, together with a large slice of bread; he then went to the beds, shook up the pillows, and made them all ready for the night. After this, feeling rather tired, he thought he would lie down and rest. He did not, however, venture to occupy either of the beds, but threw himself down on some mats that lay in a corner, carefully pulling one over him.

After lying awake for some time, Thorstein was just dropping off to sleep when he heard loud underground rumblings. Presently the door was thrown open, and he heard heavy steps crossing the floor.

Then a loud, gruff voice exclaimed : " Some one has been here ! but whoever it is, we shall soon put an end to him."

" No," answered another voice, "that you shall not do ! I take him, whoever it may be, under my protection ; I have the right to do this, for it is my turn, and can dispose of him as I like. He came here of his own free will, and has shown himself both able and willing to be useful. He has made our beds, prepared our food, and all has been well done. Let him now show himself and no harm shall befall him."

When Thorstein heard these words, he once again began to breathe freely, and throwing back the rug he had drawn over him, stood up before them.

The young men were regular giants, both in size and strength, especially the elder, who had taken his part, and who was quite a head taller than his brother.

Thorstein then went to fetch another plate and cup, and shared in the giants' meal, after which the two brothers retired to their beds, Thorstein again taking possession of his rugs, where he soon fell soundly asleep, never waking till long after the sun had risen.

Then, while they were at breakfast, the elder giant, whose name was Osric, asked Thorstein whether he would stay on with them; that all he would have to do would be to get their meals ready for them and make their beds. He might also keep his horses in their stables; and as to food and wine, Thorstein would only have to tell them what was needed, and they would always keep the larder and cellar filled, so that Thorstein need never leave the hill.

Thorstein said he would try it for a week. At the end of that time the giants were so well pleased with him, that they urged him to remain with them, for a year, at any rate ; and though Thorstein found the life rather dull and stupid, he agreed to stop, Osric, the elder giant, promising him a rich reward at the end of his term. He then handed him the keys of all the rooms in the house, except one key, and this the giant always wore fastened to a string round his neck, only taking it off at night when he went to bed.

When the two brothers had gone off on their daily expeditions, Thorstein made a regular round of the house, looking into the storerooms, cellars, and every room except the one of which Osric kept the key. In vain he tried all the keys on his bunch, hoping one of them might open the lock ; but in vain. He then tried to force open the door by throwing himself against it with all his might ; but in this also he failed

Later on, Thorstein noticed that Osric always went into this room every night and morning, while Bifrou, the younger giant, waited for him outside. So one day he asked Osric why, when handing him the keys of all the other rooms, he had kept back this one.

" Surely," he continued, " if you have found me faithful in all you have entrusted me with, you might also trust me with what is in that room."

But Osric said there was really nothing particular

in the room. Thorstein might be quite sure of that, for, having found him so faithful and honest respecting everything placed under his care, they would certainly also have trusted him if there had been anything valuable in the room.

But although Thorstein pretended that he was quite satisfied with the giant's answer, he made up his mind to solve the mystery in some way.

At length the end of the year arrived, and the two giant brothers, well pleased to have secured so careful a servant, gave him as his wages two great sacks filled with gold. They had never been made so comfortable before, and again begged Thorstein to remain another year.

To this Thorstein would not agree, but said he would remain six months, as he was more than ever determined to find out the mystery of the locked room.

He therefore carefully watched every opportunity, hoping Osric might perhaps by chance leave the key behind him. But the giant was much too careful to do so.

One morning, when Thorstein had risen particularly early, in order to bake the bread, the thought of the locked chamber came constantly before him, and while kneading the dough he kept puzzling his head as to how he could circumvent the giant.

Suddenly a bright idea struck him. Creeping softly to the back door, which led into the stable yard, he gave a loud knock, and then ran back as quickly as he could to the room where the giants were sleeping, and asked them, with a scared face (holding the dough he had been kneading in his hands), whether they had not heard some one knocking.

" Oh, yes," they both replied; " we did hear something, but we thought it was you knocking down a chair while you were sweeping."

Thorstein declared he had not knocked down anything, and added that he was afraid to open the door, for he was quite positive some one had knocked there.

The giants said he was quite right not to open it, for it might be some unfriendly giant; so they got up themselves, and ran to the door to see who had disturbed them at that early hour in the morning.

No sooner had they left the room than Thorstein drew forth the key of the mysterious chamber, which the biggest giant always kept under his pillow at night, and quickly taking an impression of it in the dough he had in his hand, replaced the key in its former place.

When the brothers came back they were not a little put out, for of course they found no one at the door, and declared that Thorstein had only said it in order to make fun of them.

But this Thorstein denied stoutly, and maintained that he had heard some one knocking, and supposed, whoever it was, must have run away.

"HE SAW A YOUNG GIRL FASTENED TO A NAIL IN THE WALL
BY HER LONG PLAITS OF HAIR."—Page 53.

Icelandic Fairy Tales.

CHAPTER III.

THE MYSTERY OF THE LOCKED ROOM.

As soon as the giants had gone forth that day to seek for treasure, as usual, Thorstein tried to make a key at the giants' forge from the impression he had taken in the dough ; but many and fruitless were the trials ere he succeeded. Then, watching his opportunity, when the brothers had gone on a long expedition, he unlocked the forbidden door, and entered the mysterious chamber.

At first he could see nothing, for it was almost dark, the single window being heavily barred and shuttered. But having struck a light, he glanced eagerly round. There, to his amazement and horror, he saw a young girl fastened to a nail in the wall by her long plaits of hair.

Mounting on a chair, he hastened to release her, and begged her to tell him who she was, and how and why she had come there.

At first the poor girl could scarcely believe that she had at last found a friend ; but Thorstein looked so good and kind, that her fears quickly vanished.

"Alas!" she said, "I am a most unhappy maiden! My name is Thekla, and my father is King Alfhelm. One day, as I was playing in a field near the palace with my maidens, a great giant suddenly rushed in among us from the neighboring wood, and snatching me up in his arms, despite all my cries and struggles, carried me down to the shore, where his boat was waiting. Ere any help could reach us, we were well out of sight, till at length we arrived at this place. He then asked me to marry him, which I indignantly refused to do; and though he comes every day to try and persuade me to consent, I will *never* give in; no, not though they starve or kill me!" And she burst again into bitter sobs.

Thorstein tried to comfort her as best he could. He told her that, having now made a key, he would be able to come and see her every day while the giants were away. He then brought her some food, for the poor girl was half starved (as the giant only gave her just enough to keep her alive), and then, as evening drew near, Thorstein again fastened Thekla's hair to the nail, ere he closed the door before the giants' return.

From that day forward Thorstein visited the poor girl regularly every day, always bringing her some food, and then putting all straight again ere the brothers returned, so that they had no idea of what took place during their absence.

When the end of the six months drew near, Thorstein told the giants that he wished to leave. But they had got so used to him, and he waited on them so carefully, that they did not want to part with him, and begged him to remain another year.

At first Thorstein refused, but after much persuasion, the brothers giving him again two more sacks of gold as wages, Thorstein said he would remain another six months, if at the end of that time they would give him as wages whatever was in the locked room—no matter whether it was valuable or not.

When Osric heard this he grew very angry, and told Thorstein not to be a fool; that what he was asking for was utterly worthless; and that he had much better accept the good wages they were quite willing to give him.

Thorstein, however, would not give in. He said he did not care whether the contents of the room were valuable or not. He had set his heart upon that, and nothing else, and would remain with them on no other condition.

Osric grew furious, and they argued and fought over this, till at last Bifrou, seeing that Thorstein was quite determined, advised his brother to give in, for they could keep him in no other way. So the big giant at last agreed to his terms.

During the six months that followed, Thorstein did his utmost to lighten Thekla's imprisonment. Many a long and pleasant chat they had together, planning their future life, while Thekla described her former home, and how delighted her father would be to see her safely back again.

At length the weary six months came to an end; and though the giant brothers again tried to persuade Thorstein to remain with them, he was firm, and would listen to no further promises of future wealth and greatness with which they tried to bribe him.

So, seeing that neither persuasions nor threats would prevail, Osric at last opened the door and brought out Thekla; very much surprised he was to see her looking so well when he saw her in the daylight, and half repented him of his promise.

But Thorstein led forth his two horses, which he had all this time carefully groomed and tended. Placing two sacks of gold on each, he lifted Thekla on one horse, and buckling on his sword, as well as a sharp dagger, mounted the other horse.

As he did so, Thekla noticed the giants whispering together, and heard the younger one mutter, with a laugh, "Yes, as soon as they get to the ravine."

"Oh, Thorstein," she said, when they had ridden on a short distance, "I know they mean to attack us. I heard them say so."

"Never fear," replied Thorstein. "My good sword has never failed me yet! But you ride on in front."

As soon as they were out of sight, he placed the other sacks of gold on Thekla's horse, and bidding her ride on ahead, he drew his sword and kept a keen lookout.

They rode on thus for some little distance. The country was open, and though the road was rough, they were soon out of sight of the castle. At length they arrived at the narrow ravine which led down to the shore. They had not long entered it when they heard the clatter of horses' hoofs behind them. Thorstein bade Thekla ride on. He then hid himself behind a projecting rock, and as Bifrou, who was in front, rode past, Thorstein rushed at him, and with one blow of his sword, severed his head from his body. Osric, seeing what had befallen his brother and fearing the same fate, rode back to the castle for more help.

Thorstein then joined Thekla, who had anxiously watched the combat, and they rode on, hoping that all danger of pursuit was now over. But just as they emerged from the ravine, Thorstein, looking back, saw Osric, accompanied by a still bigger and fiercer-looking giant, hurrying after them.

Again sending Thekla on in front, he turned and faced his enemies. A terrible combat now ensued. They attacked Thorstein, one on each side, but he

"HE THEN HID HIMSELF BEHIND A PROJECTING ROCK."

swung his great broadsword round his head and with one blow cut off Osric's head. Then the big giant, seeing his friend fall to the ground, grew furious. He threw away his sword, and grasping Thorstein round the waist, flung him to the ground. But in an instant Thorstein was on his feet again, and now a desperate conflict ensued. They wrestled together fiercely; sometimes one, sometimes the other was uppermost, but at length the giant's weight and size began to tell, and Thekla was horrified to see Thorstein grow pale and stagger.

Without a moment's thought or hesitation she sprang from her horse, and, snatching up the dagger that had fallen from Thorstein's girdle during the struggle, she thrust it through the heart of the giant, who rolled over on his side without a groan.

Both the giant brothers and their friend being now dead, Thorstein said they had better return to their house and take possession of all the treasure they could find. This they did, and by making several journeys backwards and forwards, they had quite a large store of boxes on the shore, filled with gold and precious stones.

Then, to their joy, they one day saw a vessel nearing the land, which, as it came closer, proved to be a ship belonging to Thekla's father, the captain, called Randur, being one of his chief ministers.

The latter was delighted when he saw Thekla, for her father had been so greatly distressed at her disappearance that he had fitted out several ships to go in search of her, promising that he would bestow her as a bride on whoever was fortunate enough to find her.

Randur therefore at once offered to take them home, and sent some of his men ashore to help and carry Thorstein's treasure down to the ship. When everything was put on board, the sails were set, and the good vessel sped gallantly on her homeward way.

CHAPTER IV.

HOW THORSTEIN'S KIND ACTIONS RECEIVED THEIR REWARD.

THEKLA and Thorstein now thought all their trials were surely over, and gave themselves up to the enjoyment of each other's society. But Randur had no intention of letting the latter reach Thekla's home. So he watched his opportunity, and one night, when they were well out at sea, he had one of the boats lowered. In this he placed Thorstein, who was fast asleep in the after-part of the ship, and, casting loose the boat, let it drift away. He then made the men take a solemn oath never to mention what had been done, but that if any one asked about Thorstein, they were to say they knew nothing about him.

Next morning, when Thekla, surprised at not seeing Thorstein, asked where he was, Randur pretended to be greatly surprised at his non-appearance, and instituted a search all over the vessel for him.

Thekla was very unhappy to think that Thorstein should have disappeared so unaccountably; then, suddenly missing one of the boats, she said that perhaps he had gone fishing, and insisted upon the vessel being put about to search for him.

But though Randur pretended to obey her orders, shifting the sails and issuing various commands, he was in reality hurrying home as fast as he could, rejoicing at having so successfully rid himself of his rival.

The boat, meanwhile, in which Thorstein lay fast asleep, had drifted a long distance from the ship ere he awoke, and on first opening his eyes he could not imagine where he was. But when he once realized his position, he decided that Randur's jealousy must have played him this trick, and he set himself to think what he had better do.

When Randur had sent him adrift, he had put neither food nor water in the boat, and as the sun rose higher and higher in the heavens, the heat grew intense. In vain he steeped his clothes in the water, hoping thus, at least, to assuage his thirst, which was causing him much suffering. He gradually grew more faint and weary, and a feeling of hopelessness was stealing over him, when suddenly he heard a voice saying, "Do not lose heart, Thorstein, though your plight is sad, drifting thus hopelessly about on the ocean. But as you once spent your all to give me rest, so now I will also aid you."

And immediately the boat flew rapidly over the

water, propelled by an unseen force. Thorstein's thirst and weariness vanished, and he reached the island where Thekla's father lived at the same time as the ship in which she was returning, though he landed at a different point.

As Thorstein stepped on shore, he again heard the strange voice, saying, " I am only repaying what I owe you, for had you not given up all you possessed to the farmer to whom I was in debt, he would never have allowed my bones to rest in peace in the grave. And now I will help you further. This is King Alfhelm's country. Go to the palace, and there offer to look after the king's chestnut horses, of which he is very proud. His late groom was very careless, and has been dismissed, so he will engage you. But, remember, whatever is found beneath the horses' mangers belongs to you, and you can keep it."

So saying, the spirit of the dead man departed, and Thorstein, having thanked him gratefully, at once started off for the king's palace.

King Alfhelm, who had been rather at a loss as to whom to entrust with his fine chestnut horses, of which he was very proud, was greatly pleased with Thorstein's appearance, and at once put him in charge of the stable, where Thorstein, to his surprise, saw his own chestnut among the other horses—

for Randur, on landing, had given it as a present to the king. But the horse would allow no strange hand to come near it; the moment it saw Thorstein, however, it became gentle as a lamb.

The king, meanwhile, was greatly rejoiced at his daughter's safe return, for he had almost given up all hope of ever seeing her again. So he ordered a great feast to be prepared to celebrate her arrival, and believing Randur's tale, that *he* had rescued the princess from the giants, promised to give him his daughter in marriage.

To this, however, Thekla objected.

"Rather than wed Randur, I will remain single all my life," she said.

This threat so frightened the king, for, having no son, he looked forward to seeing Thekla's children growing up, that he did not urge her any further.

Thekla then begged her father to summon the new groom to the great hall that evening, for she had been told that he had traveled a great deal, and it would amuse them all to hear his adventures.

So the king, willing to please his daughter, and anxious himself to hear the tale of his adventures, summoned Thorstein to the big hall, where the whole court was assembled.

And then the whole truth came to light; and when King Alfhelm heard the wickedness and treachery of his minister, he grew so angry that he ordered Ran-dur to be torn to pieces by wild horses.

But Thekla and Thorstein both interceded for him, so he was only banished for life from the kingdom.

Very soon after, the marriage of Thorstein and the fair princess was celebrated, amid general re-joicings. In addition to the treasure they had brought back from the giants' house, Thorstein, on looking under the horses' mangers, found an im-mense pile of old golden coins, rare ornaments, and precious stones, which had been hidden there in ancient war times by some previous kings.

After King Alfhelm's death, who lived long enough to see three little grandchildren running beside him, Thorstein and Thekla succeeded to the throne.

They were both greatly beloved by their people, whose lives they ever studied to make happy, so much so, that to this day that period is always spoken of as "the reign of the good king and queen."

5

SIGURD.

CHAPTER I.

SIGURD FINDS A FRIEND IN HIS STEPMOTHER.

In olden times there lived a king and queen who had an only son called Sigurd. All went happily until the boy was about ten years old, and then the queen became very ill and died. According to the custom of that land, her body was embalmed and placed on a funeral pile, and there it was watched by the king, who sat day after day beside it in inconsolable grief.

Time went on, but he refused to leave the funeral pile, and all the business of the kingdom came to a standstill, for the sovereign gave no heed to what went on around him, and the courtiers had one and all failed to influence him.

At last one day he raised his eyes from the ground and looked towards the great pine forest that stretched away as far as you could see round the palace, and there, under the trees, coming towards

66

him, he saw a most beautiful woman, her tall figure clothed in costly black robes.

"Who are you?" he asked, as she drew near.

"My name is Injibjörg," she answered, in a low, sweet voice. "Why are you sitting here alone?"

"Because the queen is dead, and my heart is filled with sorrow."

"Alas! I can sympathize with you in your grief," she replied. "I, too, lost my husband only yesterday, and now I am alone in the world."

The king for the first time began to be interested in something. Here was a person as sad as himself. They soon began talking like old friends, and in the end decided that, as they were both so lonely, it would be a wise thing for them to marry. The king invited her to return with him to the palace, and in a few days the wedding took place, amid the rejoicings of the people at the return of their sovereign once more to everyday life and work.

Under the wise influence of Injibjörg the king soon regained his usual health and spirits. He began to take up the neglected affairs of the kingdom, and rode out constantly hunting and fishing, attended by his court. And Sigurd? In his stepmother the boy found a true friend, who cared for him with a real mother's love, and made his life full of sunshine. They were inseparable companions, and people would stop and watch them as they passed along the roads, or played together in the palace gardens, saying, "Ah, the good stepmother! See how she loves the poor motherless boy." They were a pretty picture —the fair-haired, handsome little prince, and the beautiful tall woman, with her gracious manners and winning smile.

And thus their lives went happily on until Sigurd was almost a youth and as tall as his stepmother.

One evening Sigurd and Injibjörg were returning to the palace from a long stroll. The sun was lighting up the stems of the pine-trees as they walked along beneath them. He had noticed for some days that his mother, as he loved to call her, appeared sad and out of spirits, but to-day the deepest depression seemed to possess her. As they drew near home, she laid her hand lovingly on the boy's arm.

"My son, your father goes hunting to-morrow. It is my wish that you go with him and leave me alone for a day."

"But, mother, why? You are sad, I see; my place is surely with you. I love hunting, as you know, but I cannot leave you thus."

And all her persuasions were in vain.

Next morning the king set out, but the young prince remained with his stepmother, in spite of all she could say.

" Alas ! alas ! " she said, when they were left alone, " why did you disobey my wishes ? I fear me that you will repent it sorely."

Then she led Sigurd to her own room, and told him to hide under her bed until she called him forth. Directly he was safely hidden, the ground began to tremble, there was a terrific noise like thunder, and out of a great fissure appeared a huge giantess. Her feet were buried in the earth up to her ankles, for she was too tall to stand upright in the room. Through a small aperture in the hangings of the great bed, Sigurd watched to see what would happen.

" A pleasant greeting to you, Sister Injibjörg ! " he heard the giantess say. " Is Sigurd, the king's son, at home ? "

" No," replied Injibjörg. " He has gone hunting with his father."

Then the queen spread the table for her terrible giant sister, with rich and dainty dishes. When the meal was at an end, the giantess said, " I thank you for the nicest food and the best drink of mead that I have yet tasted. Is Sigurd, the king's son, at home ? "

Again Injibjörg said no. So the giantess took leave of her and departed ; the floor closed up, and all was quiet once more. Then the queen called Sigurd, embraced him with the greatest affection, and, after a short time, regained her usual cheerfulness.

When the king returned in the evening from the chase, neither the queen nor Sigurd told him what had happened during his absence.

The next morning he declared his intention of going out hunting in a still further part of the kingdom, and once more Injibjörg tried to persuade the boy to go with his father. Her persuasions were useless. He was more than ever determined to stay with her, hoping, in some unforeseen way, that he might be of use; for that there was some dreadful mystery about the giantess, he was sure.

This time, directly the king left, Injibjörg put the prince into a large press, and as she turned away, he saw tears in her eyes, and guessed that she feared some terrible new visitor. And he was right. Hardly had she closed the door when the noises of yesterday were renewed; the ground quaked, and a still greater giantess appeared, her feet buried in the floor up to her knees to allow of her entering the room.

"A pleasant greeting to you, Sister Injibjörg," she cried. "Is Sigurd, the king's son, at home?"

"No," said Injibjörg. "How should he be, when the king, his father, is hunting far from the palace?"

And, as yesterday, she immediately began to

spread the table with delicacies. When the meal was over, the giantess took her leave, saying, "I thank thee for the best food and most refreshing draught of ale that I have yet tasted. Is Sigurd, the king's son, at home?"

Again Injibjörg said no, and in a few moments she was alone, and all was quiet.

Then Sigurd came out of the press, and once more his mother clasped him in her arms, and he heard her say to herself, "My son, my son! if I can but save him once more, all may yet be well."

With tears she entreated him, for her sake, to go away with his father the next day.

"Twice I have hidden you successfully, but my third sister comes to-morrow, and she is sharper and fiercer than either of the others. If I can save you this time, they will never come again. My son, leave me this once. Even if they do me harm I shall know that you are safe."

"Mother," Sigurd answered, "I am no longer a little child. If you are in danger at all, my place is with you. And I am sure that your sister cannot do me any real harm."

CHAPTER II.

HE WRESTLES WITH THE GIANT SISTERS.

ALL that evening she tried her utmost to alter his decision, and also the next morning, for now the day had come, and brought with it a presage of evil. But nothing would move Sigurd.

Directly the king had ridden forth, Injibjörg concealed the prince behind some thick hangings on the wall. The earth quaked, terrible noises were heard, and a gigantic woman appeared, fiercer and stronger than either of the others, and so huge that only half her body rose out of the floor.

" A pleasant greeting to you, Sister Injibjörg," she cried, in a harsh, terrible voice. " Is Sigurd, the king's son, at home ? "

" No," replied Injibjörg, in a faltering voice. " He is hunting with his father in the woods."

" I see you lie ! " roared the giantess. " The boy is here ; " and she seized the queen, and began to shake her violently. But, as Injibjörg continued to protest that the prince was not at home, she relaxed her hold, and the table was spread as usual with beautiful dishes. When the meal was ended, the giantess rose. "I thank you for the best meal I have ever tasted," she said. "Is Sigurd, the king's son, at home?"

"No," replied Injibjörg. "Have I not already answered you?"

"A GIGANTIC WOMAN APPEARED."

"Aha!" cried the giantess, her wicked, malicious laugh making the rafters ring. "Then if he be so far away, my words can do him no harm. But should he be within hearing, I decree that half of his body shall wither up, and he shall never recover until he has sought and found me. And you, my sister, be thankful if a worse fate does not overtake you."

And, with another peal of mocking laughter, she disappeared.

Trembling from head to foot, the queen went to find her son; but, alas! when she led him forth from his hiding-place, the curse had fallen upon him, and his left side was shrunk and withered.

"Sigurd, Sigurd," she cried, holding him close, and weeping bitterly. "See what has happened because you would not leave me. Better far that I should have suffered than that this should have fallen upon you. Alas! alas! what shall we do?"

"Mother," he answered bravely, "there is but one thing—I must seek your sister, as she said, and perhaps, in doing that, I may chance to free you also from their dread visits forever. Tell me what I must do to find her, and let me depart at once, before my father returns, lest he see me like this, and be angry with you. I grieve to leave you; but it is best, I know. Watch for my return day by day, dear mother, and give me your blessing before I go. Your love will make me strong to bear all that may lie before me."

Then Injibjörg took a large ball of wool out of a chest and gave it to her son, with three golden rings.

"As soon as you let this ball fall to the ground,"

she said, "it will go on rolling till it reaches some rocks. Follow it till it stops, and one of the giantesses will come forth. Do not lose heart. Do whatever she wishes you to. She will draw you up on to the rock where she stands, and you must salute her, and present her with the smallest ring. When she sees the gold she will be delighted, and will challenge you to wrestle with her. When you get exhausted she will offer you a drink out of a horn; and I have prayed that the strength of that magic draught will make you the victor in the wrestling match, so that she will allow you to depart next day. My other two sisters will behave in the same manner; but be brave and fearless, and remember what I tell you. One thing, dear son, keep ever in your mind, as you love me. If at any time my dog comes suddenly to you, puts his paws on your knees, and looks up at you, while tears run down his face, hasten home, let nothing stay you, for my life will be in danger. Do not forget your stepmother Injibjörg."

Many times Sigurd embraced the queen before he at length left her on his dangerous journey. And as he looked back for a last farewell, he saw her tall, graceful figure still standing watching him at the entrance of the palace. He knew she was wondering if she should ever see her beloved son again. And his heart was very heavy at leaving her in such grief.

Directly he was out of sight of the palace, he threw the ball on the ground, and eagerly followed its winding course.

Towards sunset he found himself in a wild and rocky region, and at length the ball led him to the foot of a precipitous rock, on the summit of which sat the first giantess.

"Aha!" she cried, "this is splendid! Here is Sigurd, the king's son. He shall be my meal to-night. Come up, comrade! Come hither! Thou art not afraid of a woman, I feel sure."

With these mocking words she reached down a long boat-hook, and drew him up beside her. Sigurd greeted her bravely, and presented her with the smallest of the golden rings. When she saw the gold, the giantess was delighted. "Ah! now thou shalt wrestle with me," she cried.

And they began. Sigurd fought bravely, and when she saw him getting tired she gave him a draught of mead, which made him so strong that he came off victor in the end, and she let him go.

The next day, bidding her farewell, he again followed the ball till it reached another high rock. There sat the second giantess.

She greeted the youth in the same fashion as her

sister, pulled him up beside her, and was so delighted at the gift of the ring, that she, too, offered to wrestle with Sigurd for the victory before making her meal off him.

Again, as he got exhausted, he was offered a drink of mead from a huge horn, and was able to throw his opponent to the ground with one hand.

On the third day Sigurd rose with a lighter heart—only one more foe to meet, and then the victory would be won: his mother freed from the hateful dominion of her sisters, and he himself restored to his usual appearance. As he looked at his withered arm and leg, he vowed to use every effort to become victor.

CHAPTER III.

HIS MEETING WITH HELGA.

It was early morning when Sigurd left the home of the second giantess, but night had nearly fallen before his ball stopped at the foot of the highest rock he had yet come to. On the summit stood the huge figure he had last seen on that fatal day at the palace; her head seemed to touch the clouds, and a terrible smile played on her lips as she looked down at the prince.

"Aha! So you have followed me, as I said. Up, comrade, up! You shall have your wish, and see how you like a contest with me in person."

But Sigurd's heart did not fail him. "Draw me up," he said; "I have a message for you from my stepmother, Queen Injibjörg."

Then the giantess drew him up, as her sisters had done, and he presented the last and largest of the golden rings. This pleased her immensely, and she proposed that they should at once wrestle for the victory, without waiting any longer. Sigurd exerted his utmost strength, feeling that on this combat all his future happiness depended; and just when he thought he could hold out no longer, the giantess reached him a horn of mead, which, as before, gave him supernatural strength, and he forced her to her knees.

In a moment he felt that his withered side was healed. The glow of perfect health came over him, and he could have sung aloud and danced for joy.

" Thou hast conquered, Sigurd, the king's son," the giantess said—" conquered in fair fight. I am no longer thine enemy; my power over thee is gone forever. Now, go forth. Not far from here is a lake. There thou wilt see a maiden rocking herself in a boat. Give her this small ring, and it will be of use to thee. Thou art a brave youth, and I have done that for thee which I would not do for any one else. Thy strength is now fully restored to thee, and thou shalt succeed in all thine undertakings."

With grateful thanks, Sigurd bade her farewell, and took his way to the lake she had told him of. All through the night he went on, and when the morning sun arose he saw the glitter of its rays on the water. As he reached the shore he beheld a lovely girl in a tiny green-and-gold boat, gently rocking herself to and fro on the waves, close to the edge of the water.

Sigurd approached, doffed his cap, and ventured to ask her name.

"My name is Helga," she said, "and I live yonder with my father,"—pointing to a castle in the distance.

Then Sigurd showed her the ring he had received from the giantess.

"I have come all this way to give it to you," he said; "fate has decreed that we are to be great friends. Will you accept it and wear it always?"

"I have no friends," Helga answered. "I will gladly have you for one and wear your ring."

So he placed it on her finger, and they rowed in the little boat, and wandered about the woods on the shores of the lake, until the sun began to sink behind the hills.

"Alas!" cried Helga, as she saw the slanting rays, "it is getting late; I must away home."

"I will come too," Sigurd answered.

"No, no," she cried, in a terrified voice. "My father allows no stranger to enter our home. He would certainly kill you if he found you. No, you must not come." And she set off running.

Sigurd ran too, and came up with her just as they reached the door. Helga put out her hand, the one which bore the ring he had given her, to stop him. In a moment, the young prince had disappeared, and where he had stood there was now only a huge bundle of wool. Helga then realized that the ring he had given her was a magic one, which she must use for his protection. She at once lifted up the bundle of wool in her arms, carried it into the castle hall, and threw it up on a high shelf.

At that instant her father came striding in—he was a giant of great size. Taking no notice of his daughter, he began searching in all the corners, and finding nothing, cried out in an angry voice: "Where has he gone? What was that I saw you carrying, child?"

"Only a bundle of wool, father," Helga answered, as fearlessly as she could.

"Ah, it must have been that; but I thought I saw some one with you," he muttered, and soon after retired to his room. The next morning, when Helga went out as usual, she carried the bundle of wool with her, and when she reached the boat, she touched it with her ring, and Sigurd regained his natural form. They rowed to a more distant part of the lake, and spent another happy day together.

Sigurd told Helga all about his stepmother, and his love for her.

"I owe everything to her kindness," he said, "and I shall never be really happy till I have finished this journey and returned to her. Even when I am with you I dread lest evil may have overtaken

her in my absence. But the giantess sent me here
for some end, which I must wait to perform. My
mother is the most beautiful woman I have ever
seen, except you."

Helga, in her turn, told him of her lonely life
with her fierce old father, and of how she had always longed to have some one of her own age as a
companion.

"But what shall I do when I am left alone
again?" she asked, with tears in her eyes.

"Be comforted," Sigurd said, as he took her
hand in his. "I must return to my stepmother,
but I will come again, and take you away with me
to my own home."

As they returned, Helga said: "To-morrow we
shall have more freedom, for my father goes to a
great gathering of giants, and I will show you over
the castle in his absence." When they reached the
house, Helga touched him with her ring, and once
again Sigurd became a bundle of wool, and passed
the night on a shelf in the hall.

Next morning, almost at break of day, Helga's
father departed, and Sigurd was enabled to resume
his natural form at once. They walked and talked
for some time, and then Sigurd reminded Helga of
her promise to show him over the castle. She produced a huge bunch of keys, and together they

passed through room after room, each one more beautiful than the last.

"And what is that key for?" asked the prince, pointing to a very strange one, which Helga had not yet used.

"That is my father's secret room. The key is of a different pattern to all the others."

"It is, indeed. But surely you will not refuse to let me see that room also?" And as he spoke, they passed to a door strongly studded with great iron nails. He entreated Helga not to refuse his request. "This, 1 am sure, is the door."

"Yes, you are right. But if I open the door you must only just peep in, for I myself am terrified to go inside."

"Nothing can hurt you while you are with me," Sigurd said, placing his arm round her; and, with trembling fingers, Helga fitted the key into the massive lock, and opened the door a couple of inches. But Sigurd pushed it wide open and boldly stood in the doorway. There he saw a magnificent horse, richly caparisoned, eating golden hay, while, suspended to the rafters above its head, hung a sword sheathed in gold, with these words engraved on the hilt—

Whoever mounts this horse, and is armed with this sword, good luck will ride with him.

Sigurd entreated Helga to let him ride the horse once round the castle, and to carry the sword in his hand. At first Helga would not hear of it. Something terrible would happen, she felt sure. But the young prince pleaded so irresistibly, that at last he won her reluctant consent. The horse, she told him, was called Gullfaxi, " the golden mane "; the sword, Gunnfjöden, "fighting blade."

CHAPTER IV.

HIS ESCAPE ON THE WONDERFUL HORSE GULLFAXI.

SIGURD led the beautiful steed outside the castle, took down the sword, and had just mounted, when Helga came running to him with something in her hand.

"Here, I give you a green branch, a stone, and a stick," she said, "else I fear that you may get into trouble. Listen carefully to what I tell you. If, when you are mounted on the horse, an enemy should follow you and threaten to take your life, you have only to throw down the green branch as you ride along, and immediately a dense forest will grow up behind you. Should the enemy still attempt to follow, you have only to strike the stick on the white stone, and a terrible hailstorm will kill all who come after you."

As she finished speaking, and Sigurd gathered up the reins to start off, Helga gave a cry of terror. Striding over the brow of the hill, she saw the huge form of her father.

"Fly! fly!" she said. "Use the steed for your

own protection; it is your only chance of life. Save
yourself, for my sake."

Raising his cap in farewell to his young hostess,
Sigurd set spurs to Gullfaxi, and as the noble ani-

"HELGA GAVE A CRY OF TERROR."

mal put forth his full speed, the prince turned in
the saddle and shook his fist at the angry giant.

Without staying to question his daughter, the
giant strode after his horse, breathing out threats of
vengeance. At first he could only just keep them
in sight; but, with his gigantic strides, he soon began to gain upon them when the ground grew rocky

and hilly. Then Sigurd threw down Helga's green branch, and immediately a thick forest rose between him and his enemy.

But the giant seized his ax, and began with mighty strokes to hew his way through the wood. Crash went trees and bushes; crash, crash, to right and to left, and when Sigurd looked back a second time, the giant was through the forest, and close behind him. Then Sigurd touched the white stone with his stick, and immediately such a terrible hail-storm broke loose behind him that the giant was killed on the spot, while Sigurd rode on in bright sunshine.

The giant dead, Sigurd thought he would return and fetch Helga; but while he was debating which road to take, he saw his stepmother's dog running towards him. The dog was dusty and footsore, and whined piteously as he drew near. Sigurd dismounted, and went to meet him; the dog put his paws upon the prince's knee, and looked up at him with tears running down his face. Then Sigurd's heart was very heavy, for he knew misfortune was threatening his beloved stepmother. He leapt on to his horse, and rode at full speed, taking no rest, either by day or night, till at length he came out of the thick pinewoods, and saw the palace before him. In the courtyard a great crowd was assembled, and there, fastened to a stake, and surrounded by huge fagots, he saw the graceful figure of his stepmother.

"Here is Sigurd—Sigurd, the king's lost son," he heard voices say, as if in a dream, as he galloped furiously on.

He, however, saw nothing but the beautiful pale face of the queen as he leaped from his horse, and pushed his way through the crowd, sword in hand. He cut the bands with which Injibjörg was fastened, scattered the guards, and carried her into the palace, to his father's room.

There he found the king lying on his couch, sick unto death for grief at the loss of his son.

"My father," Sigurd cried, as he stood before him with his arm round his stepmother, "what is this that has been done? Why has my mother been treated thus in my absence?"

"My son," his father cried, hardly believing that he saw him alive and well before him, "where hast thou been? The people declared the queen had taken thy life, and she was therefore condemned to death, while I was too ill to save her from their vengeance. Forgive me, Sigurd, and beg the queen also to pardon me;" and he embraced them both with the utmost affection.

Then Sigurd related all his adventures, and how he had freed Injibjörg forever from the hateful power of her sisters. His love for his stepmother was greater than ever, as he heard of all that she had suffered in his absence. He was not happy now when she was out of his sight, and he tried in every way to make up to her for what had passed. He told her, too, of Helga in the castle by the lake; and when she was quite restored to health, he set out, with her blessing and that of his father, to fetch the maiden to his home, as he had promised.

Helga was rejoiced to see Sigurd again, for she had watched for him day by day. They brought away all the treasures of the castle, and in a short time there was a magnificent wedding between Helga and Sigurd, the marriage feast lasting a whole month.

When the king died, Sigurd and Helga came to the throne, and, guided by the wise counsels of Injibjörg, the kingdom became renowned far and near for its good rule and the happiness of its people.

LINEIK AND LAUFEY.

In olden days, there once lived a king called Ring, and his queen Gytha, who reigned over a mighty kingdom. They had two children, a son and a daughter, who were both almost grown up when my story begins. The boy was called Siegfrid, and the daughter Lineik. They were both as beautiful in person as they were gifted in mind. No one in the whole kingdom was their equal; and they loved each other so dearly that the one was never happy when the other one was away. Their father, therefore, had a beautiful palace built for them, where they had as many servants as they wanted, and everything they could possibly wish for.

Here the brother and sister lived together very happily until the queen fell ill, and feeling her end was drawing near, she called the king to her bedside.

"Dear husband," she said, " we have lived very happily together ; but now my end is drawing near, and, before I die, I hope you will grant two requests I wish to make—first, if ever you marry again, do

not choose your wife from any small village or lonely
island, but bring your bride from one of the large
cities in the neighboring kingdoms. If you do this,
good fortune will attend you. Secondly, never let
any one or anything come between you and our
dear children; they will bring you good luck and
happiness if you always let them stand first in your
love and affection."

When the queen had spoken these words, she lay
back and died. The king was very grieved at her
death. He sorrowed so greatly that he never left
his room and would not see any one, and all the
affairs of the kingdom came to a standstill.

Then one day the prime minister came to him,
and told him that there would be a rebellion, and
that the country would go to ruin if he continued to
shut himself up instead of attending to the affairs of
his kingdom.

"It is far more kingly" he concluded, "to pull
yourself together, and try and overcome your grief
for the sake of your people, than to sit alone and
lament! Besides, why should you not look around
for another queen, who will be worthy to succeed
your late consort?"

"Alas! that will be no easy task," said the king,
sighing deeply. "I will not, however, gainsay your
words. As, however, such is your advice, it is best

that the responsibility of the choice should also be
yours. I therefore empower you to find me a bride
worthy to share my throne, and be a successor to
my late wife. I only make one stipulation : you
must not seek her in any small village or lonely
island, but from some large neighboring state."

The minister, delighted that he had at last roused
the king, and filled with the importance of his mis-
sion, promised to bear in mind the king's instructions, and set about preparing for the journey.
The king provided him with a magnificent outfit,
and a large and imposing following, and started him
on his journey.

When they had sailed for about three days on
their way to the neighboring kingdom, suddenly a
thick white fog arose ; they could no longer see
where they were going, and for a whole month they
sailed about first in one direction, then in another,
for they had lost all reckoning. Whichever way
they steered their vessels, no land was in sight, and
they were beginning to lose all heart, when at length
one day they saw a faint gray line on the horizon ;
gradually, as they came nearer, they could distinguish hills and trees, and finding a nice gently shelv-
ing beach in a sheltered nook, they ran their boats
ashore, and landing, pitched their tents on the strand.
But not a single human being was in sight, all was

perfectly still, and they thought they must have landed on a desert island.

While the men, tired with their exertions, were resting, the minister decided to go on a little way inland and explore; and as the sun was now very hot, for it was about mid-day, he bent his steps towards a forest he saw some little way ahead. He had not gone very long in that direction, when he suddenly heard a harp being played ; following the sound, he came to an open glade, and there, sitting on a fallen tree, he saw a beautiful woman, so grand, so stately, he thought he had never before seen any one so enchanting. Her playing on the harp was so perfect, that it was happiness only to listen to her, while at her feet sat the loveliest maiden he had ever seen, whose sweet voice accompanied the harpist.

The prime minister doffed his hat and bowed courteously to the lady, who, on seeing him approach, rose and returned his greeting with much friendliness, asking him where he was going and what was the object of his journey.

The minister, quite charmed with her kindness, told her the purpose of his coming.

" How strange !" said the lady, "for almost the same thing has happened to me. I, too, have lost my husband. He was one of the great kings who

reigned on this continent; but, alas! one sad day
the Vikings came, they overran the whole land,
killed my husband, and took possession of this country. It was only with great difficulty, and not
without much danger, that I managed to escape with
this maiden, who is my daughter."

When the girl heard this, she said softly—

"Is that the truth you are speaking?"

A sharp slap on the ear, while the minister was
looking at the harp, rewarded the girl's speech.

"Don't forget what I told you," muttered the
lady.

The prime minister, who had not noticed anything, now asked the lady what her name was, and
whether he could do anything for her.

"I am called Blauvör," she replied, "and my
daughter's name is Laufey."

Then the minister sat down beside her and began
to talk to her. Finding her very clever and well-
informed, and fearing that if he went further he
might fare worse, he thought he could not do better
than secure so wise and beautiful a wife for the
king; so he made proposals for her hand in his
master's name. His embassy seemed very welcome
to Blauvör, who said she would be quite willing to
accompany him, and that there need be no delay,
" for I have all my treasures here with me, and shall

not require any attendants beyond my daughter Laufey."

And so, without loss of time, the minister conducted Blauvör and Laufey to the shore. The tents were struck, and the whole party having got on board again, the sails were set and the ships turned homeward.

The dense fog which had accompanied them was now quite dispersed, and they saw that they had landed on a small rocky island ; but all were too delighted at the thoughts of the homeward journey to take any notice of this.

A fine fresh wind drove the vessels merrily along, and after six days' delightful sailing, they came in sight of land, and soon recognized the great high towers of the king's castle. Then the anchors were dropped, and they speedily began to disembark, the minister at once sending a message to King Ring, to announce their arrival.

The king was delighted to hear that his minister had been so successful. He at once put on his grandest robes of state, and, accompanied by his chief ministers and all the principal courtiers, equally richly attired, he proceeded down to the shore to receive and welcome his bride.

He had only gone half-way when he met his prime minister, leading two beautiful women by the hand.

Both were richly dressed in gold-embroidered robes, and decked with rare jewels. When King Ring saw all this richness and beauty, he was delighted beyond measure, and when he was told that the elder and the most beautiful of the two was his destined bride, he thought himself the most fortunate of kings.

He thanked the minister warmly for what he had done, and in his joyful greeting of mother and daughter, he quite forgot to ask whence his bride and her daughter had come, but led them with great pomp into the city, and lodged them in the most magnificent rooms in the palace.

A grand wedding-feast was speedily arranged, and all the great people in the kingdom were invited, only Siegfrid and Lineik were not asked. The king was so engrossed with his beautiful bride, sitting beside her and talking to her, that he had completely forgotten them.

The wedding was one of the grandest that had ever been seen, and after this feast, all the guests received rich gifts ere they departed, and then at the end of the week the king began again to look after the affairs of his kingdom.

Thus some time passed quietly, the queen was always present when the king received his ministers, and though she never said much, whispers soon went abroad that matters were not as they should be. The queen wished everything to be done her way, and insisted on hearing all that was being arranged, so that King Ring began to think that his marriage was not, after all, such a great piece of luck as he had at first imagined.

As for Siegfrid and Lineik, the queen never asked about them, nor did she see them. They never came to the palace, but kept to their own house and grounds.

Then, after a time, some of the people about the court began to disappear. No one could find out where they had gone, or what had become of them, and it was always those who had opposed the queen in the council. The king, thinking they had gone away because they would not agree to the queen's wishes, at first took no notice of these strange disappearances, but appointed other ministers in their place; and so things went on for some time.

Then one day the queen came to the king and said she thought it was time for him to make his journey through the country to collect the revenue.

" I have helped you so much in all your business that I can easily carry on the government while you are away, so you need not hurry home, but take your time and enjoy yourself," she added.

The king did not much care to go away. He was

7

getting old, and thought his prime minister might well have gone in his stead, but he was falling each day more under the queen's rule. She was the one who settled and decided everything, and if any one ventured to oppose her they were made to rue it.

The king therefore fitted out his ships for the journey, but he was very sorrowful and sad at heart. When everything was ready for him to start, he went to the house of his two children, where of late he had seldom been. A warm greeting welcomed him, and both Siegfrid and Lineik could not make enough of their father.

When the time for bidding them farewell drew near, the king grew very sad again, and sighing deeply, said—

"I cannot tell you, my children, what a sad foreboding haunts me that some evil threatens you. If I should not return from this journey, I fear it will not be safe for you to remain here. Take my advice therefore, and go away secretly, as soon as you are sure that there is no hope of my return. When you start, remember you must go towards the East —you will then soon arrive at a high, steep rock; when you have climbed this rock you will come to a long, narrow valley. Follow this valley till you come to two beautiful trees; the one has bright, glossy green leaves, the other dark bronze ones. They are hollow, and so arranged that they can be securely fastened from the inside, the opening being invisible from the outside. You must each get into one of these trees, and as long as you remain in them, nothing can touch you."

Then the king took a tender farewell of his children, and getting on board his ship, the sails were unfurled, and he started off on his journey. They had not, however, been long at sea, before a frightful storm arose. Peals of thunder rent the air, the lightning flashed incessantly, and the wind and rain lashed the sea till the waves rose mountains high and engulfed the ships, so that the king and all on board the ships were drowned.

That same night of the storm, Prince Siegfrid had a strange dream. He saw his father standing beside his bed, his clothes streaming with water. Bending over his son, he took the crown off his head and placed it beside Siegfrid on the pillow, and then passed silently away.

When Siegfrid awoke next morning, he told Lineik his dream, and they both agreed that this could only be a warning from their father, telling them of his death at sea.

They therefore quickly gathered together all their clothes and jewels, and ere the sun had fully risen,

they were well on their way on the road their father
had told them of.

When they reached the foot of the hill they looked
back, and there they beheld their stepmother in the

"SHE APPEARED MORE LIKE SOME TERRIBLE GIANTESS."

distance, following them. She looked so fierce and
angry, and so big, that she appeared more like some
terrible giantess than an ordinary woman. Fortunately they had passed the wood at the foot of the

hill, so they set fire to this, and the flames rose so quickly and brightly that their stepmother was unable to pass it, and had to go round. This gave Siegfrid and his sister time to get up the hill, but it was a long and weary climb, and once or twice Lineik was fain to sit down, but Siegfrid took her up in his arms and carried her till she was again able to walk. At last they reached the narrow valley in which stood the two trees their father had told them of. Lineik chose the one with the bronze-colored leaves, and Siegfrid, having seen her safely fastened in, got into the other tree, drawing the opening to after him. But though no one could look into the trees, the rough, thick bark grew in such cunning twists and turns, that those inside could see everything that happened outside, and the brother and sister were thus able to talk to one another.

About this time there reigned a great and power-ful king in Greece, called Menelaus. He had two children, a son called Tellus, and a daughter called Hebe. They were beautiful, clever, and good, and it would have been difficult to find their equals in all the land.

When Tellus grew to man's estate, he distinguished himself by many brave and noble deeds during his numerous warlike expeditions, which often carried him far away into foreign lands, and while thus traveling in search of adventures, he had more than once heard of Princess Lineik, who, it was said, surpassed all other women in beauty, wit, and goodness; so he determined to try and win her for his bride.

When he neared the island of King Ring, the wicked queen, who by her enchantments was aware of his coming and also his reasons for so doing, prepared to receive him with all honor. Dressing herself in her most magnificent garments, she ordered Laufey to do the same, and then went down to the shore with her maidens to receive him.

The prince, on landing, greeted her with great respect, and asked after King Ring, whereupon the queen, drawing forth her handkerchief, pretended to wipe away her tears, and told him that the king and all his attendants had perished at sea in a frightful gale, and declared she could never get over her great loss.

"And where is Princess Lineik?" asked Tellus.

"This is my dear step-daughter," replied the queen, drawing Laufey forward, who, ashamed and angry, had kept in the background.

The prince seemed much surprised, for though Laufey was very pretty, yet from the fame of Lineik's beauty he had pictured the latter as much handsomer.

But the queen, seeing his disappointment, said he must not be surprised that the dear child looked pale and sad, having lost both father and brother at one blow.

Prince Tellus thought this was but natural, so he formally demanded the princess's hand in marriage. As may well be imagined, he did not meet with any opposition from the queen, who said she would hurry on the preparations, but Prince Tellus said he had promised his father that the marriage should take place in Greece, with all due splendor, and that the princess must therefore return with him.

The queen offered to accompany them, but this the prince would not consent to. So Laufey and her maidens were escorted to the prince's ship, and they set sail for Greece, leaving Brunhild behind, greatly to her chagrin.

They had not sailed far, when a dense white mist overtook them. The steersman lost his reckoning, and when at length the fog lifted, they found they had sailed up a beautiful fiord. The mountains with their snowy tops rose steeply on each side at the entrance, but as they got further in, the fiord widened, and grassy slopes shelved down to the golden sands.

The prince ordered a boat to be lowered, and getting in, they rowed on till they came to the entrance of a narrow valley in which stood two beautiful trees.

The prince landed to look at them. He had never seen anything like them before, and nothing would satisfy him but to have them cut down and carried on board his ship to take back to Greece.

No sooner were they brought on board than the fog lifted. The sails were immediately unfurled, and the homeward journey was speedily effected.

On his arrival, Prince Tellus at once led Laufey to the palace, where she was received with all honor. He gave her up his own magnificent rooms, which looked on the court where the great fountains played and the beautiful doves circled amid the fruit and flower-laden trees and shrubs. Here Laufey was to spend her days, while at night she retired to the women's apartments under the care of the queen.

The two beautiful trees, however, Prince Tellus declared he could not part from; so he had them placed in his room, one at the head and the other at the foot of his couch.

Meanwhile the preparations for the wedding went on apace.

The prince, according to the custom of the country, then brought Laufey (believing she was Lineik) three pieces of rich silk, to make three tunics; one was blue, the other was red, and the third one was green. She was to make up the blue one first, then the red one, and last of all the green one, which was to surpass both the others in richness and beauty of design. "For," added the prince, "the green one is the one I shall wear on our wedding-day."

Laufey took the three bits of stuff, and the prince departed. But no sooner had he closed the door than, sitting down on the couch between the two trees, she burst into tears.

Oh! what was she to do? Brunhild had never taught Laufey anything, but just let her grow up as she would, so how could she, who had never had a needle in her hand, make up or embroider these beautiful stuffs? And if the prince discovered how ignorant she was, would he not send her away with scorn and laughter, or perhaps even have her put to death for her deception?

And the poor girl sobbed and cried as if her heart would break.

Now, as has already been mentioned, Siegfrid and Lineik were inside the two beautiful trees. They could therefore see all that passed in the prince's chamber, and when they heard poor Laufey's lamentations, Siegfrid was so touched at sight of the girl's tears that he said to his sister—

> " Sister Lineik,
>   Laufey weeps ;
> Oh, have pity on her,
>   And assist her with her task."

Then Lineik replied—

> " Hast thou forgotten, oh brother,
>   All Brunhild's wicked deeds,
> And how she endeavored
>   To kill both you and me ? "

But after a while Lineik consented, and creeping forth from her tree, greatly to Laufey's surprise, she told her who she was and how she came there.   Then sitting down beside her, helped her so effectually with her skilful fingers that the tunic was soon completed, greatly to Laufey's delight.   Lineik crept back into her tree, and when Prince Tellus appeared, she showed him the garment.

" I have never seen so prettily worked a tunic," he said, greatly pleased.   " Now take the piece of red silk and let that be as much more finely embroidered as the stuff itself is richer."

But when Laufey found herself confronted with this fresh piece of work, all her courage fled.   How could she carry out the prince's wishes ?   And she began to cry.

Then Siegfrid again called to his sister—

> " Sister Lineik,
>   Laufey weeps ;
> Oh, have pity on her,
>   And assist her with her task."

And again Lineik answered—

> "Hast thou forgotten, oh brother,
> Brunhild's wicked deeds,
> And how she used all endeavors
> To kill both you and me?"

Nevertheless, after a while she again consented to help Laufey, and leaving her tree she sat down beside her, cut out and made up the red tunic, devoting even more care and skill than on the first one. All the seams were embroidered in gold thread, and precious stones bordered the neck and skirt.

When it was ready she gave it to Laufey, while she herself slipped back into her tree.

Prince Tellus was greatly pleased when he saw the second tunic.

"Why, this is more beautifully worked than the first tunic! I can hardly imagine how you have done it without any one to help you. Now you must make the third and last tunic. I will give you three days to finish it; and remember that this tunic must surpass both the others in beauty of design and richness of embroidery, for I shall wear it on our wedding-day."

After the prince had gone, Laufey sat down on the couch, and felt very sad. How could she hope that Lineik would again help her? She had done

so twice, notwithstanding all the ill the queen had
intended against her and Siegfrid, and it was too
much to expect her to aid her again, and, thinking
thus sadly, the tears streamed down her cheeks.

But Prince Siegfrid was so touched by the poor
girl's grief that he again said to his sister—

> "Lineik, sister,
> Laufey weeps!
> Oh, have pity on her,
> And assist her with her task!"

And again Lineik replied—

> "Hast thou forgotten, oh brother,
> All Brunhild's wicked deeds,
> And how she used all her arts
> To kill both you and me?"

Nevertheless, after a while, she again consented
to help Laufey, and leaving her tree, she sat down
beside her, and with her deft, clever fingers the work
made rapid progress, and seemed to grow under her
hands. This time she spent even more care and
skill on the garment, and when, on the third day, it
was finished, there was hardly any portion of the
original stuff visible, so thickly was it covered with
rich gold and silver scrolls and flowers, starred with
rare and precious stones. Lineik and Laufey were
so occupied admiring their work, as they sat together
on the couch, that they did not hear the lifting of

the curtain behind them, as Prince Tellus suddenly entered the room.

Lineik, with a cry, started up hastily, and was about to slip back into her tree; but the prince sprang after her, and taking hold of both her hands, led her back to the couch, where Laufey sat in fear and trembling.

"I have long had my suspicions that some mystery was at work here," he then said; and, seating himself between the two girls, he continued, "Nay, do not fear me, but"—turning to Lineik—"tell me your name, and who you are, and how you came here."

So Lineik told him who she was, and all about her home, and how she and her brother Siegfrid had come in his ship. And as he sat and listened to her, Prince Tellus thought he had never seen any one so beautiful and clever as Lineik; she was just like what he had always pictured her to himself. Then, casting an angry glance at Laufey, he told her she deserved to be put to death for her deception of him.

Then Laufey threw herself on her knees before him, and prayed for forgiveness, in which Lineik joined most heartily.

"I only deceived you about the work of the tunics," continued Laufey; "for Lineik forbade me to say who had really worked them. You may remember that I never said I was Princess Lineik. It was Queen Brunhild—my mother, as she called herself—who thus deceived you."

And while they were thus talking, Prince Siegfrid came forth from his tree, whereupon there were fresh explanations and much rejoicing that the mystery was explained; and Prince Tellus lost no time in claiming the hand of the rightful Princess Lineik. But Lineik said she could not promise to marry any one till her wicked stepmother, who had wrought such ill to every one, was driven forth from the kingdom she had usurped.

And now Laufey had a wondrous tale to tell. Brunhild was no queen, but a wicked ogress, who reigned over the lonely island, where the Prime Minister had found her. There she had lived in a huge cave, together with other giants and ogres.

"I also am a king's daughter," continued Laufey. "But Brunhild, with great skill and cunning, stole me away one day when I was playing in the fields with my little companions. She threatened to kill me if I did not obey her in everything, and called me her daughter, for she thought people would then imagine she also came of a kingly race. It was she who killed your father," continued Laufey, turning to Siegfrid, "and all those people at your court who disappeared so mysteriously were eaten by her at night; for all ogres love human flesh. Her object was to get rid of all your chief people, and then bring over her friends the giants from the stony island, so that they might all live in your rich and fruitful kingdom."

When they had heard this tale, Siegfrid said he must at once return home and save his country from the giants. Prince Tellus declared he would accompany him, for it was an adventure quite after his own heart. So they got together a large force, and setting sail, a favorable wind speedily brought them to the island, where they landed, and surrounded the castle before Brunhild had even heard of their arrival; for very few people were about, the greater portion having been killed by Brunhild, and the rest having fled and hidden themselves to escape from the wicked queen.

So there was but little attempt at defense, and Brunhild was taken prisoner. When she saw that her wicked plans had been discovered, and that there was no hope of escape, she screamed and raved like a madwoman. But her wicked deeds deserved no pardon. She was condemned to death, and her head cut off, after which her body was burnt on a huge funeral pile in the yard of the castle.

Then the two princes returned to Greece, and a

very gay and splendid double-wedding took place, at which all the greatest nobles of the kingdom took part; for on his return, Siegfrid, who during the test of the tunics had lost his heart to Laufey, now proposed for her hand.

After the festivities were over, he and his fair bride returned to his island, and great were the rejoicings that the kingdom was again under the rule of a just and kind sovereign. He and Laufey reigned long and happily, and visits were often interchanged between them and Prince Tellus and his bride Lineik. who in time became known as the wisest and best among all the rulers of Greece.

THE FIVE BROTHERS.

ONCE upon a time, long years ago, when giants still lived upon the earth, there dwelt an old man and his wife in a small wooden hut, sheltered from the rough winter winds by the tall mountains and rocks that surrounded it. The world would have said they were very poor; but they thought themselves rich, for they had five handsome, healthy boys, who were the delight of their eyes. There was only a year's difference in age between the lads, and they were always together.

One day, the old couple went to cut grass on a slope some distance off, leaving the boys alone at home. It was a bright, warm morning and, tired of playing indoors, the children went out into the little garden, and soon their merry shouts were heard echoing from the hills. Presently, up the path towards them came an old woman, feeble and lame.

"May an old woman beg for a draught of water?" she said, in a weak voice.

Stopping their games at once, the eldest boy ran

to the well, while the others made her sit down by
the door and rest.   In a moment he was back with
a pitcher of cool, sparkling water.

"There, grannie," he said, "that will refresh you.
I let the bucket run down ever so far, to make the
water nice and cold."

The old dame thanked him heartily, and, having
quenched her thirst, asked what their names were.
The boys laughed merrily.

"We have no names," they said.   "We are all so
near in age that we do everything together; and
when father or mother want anything they just call
out 'Boys!' and there we are, always at hand."

"You have kind hearts," the old woman said;
"you are good to the aged and feeble.   I was nearly
dying of thirst, and could not have gone further
without your help.   Would that I could reward you
as I should like! Alas! I have not the power.   But
one thing I can do for you.   You shall no longer be
nameless.   I am going to bestow a name on each.
You, my young cup-bearer," turning to the eldest
boy, "shall be called 'Watchwell;' your brothers,
'Holdwell,' 'Hitwell,' 'Spywell,' and 'Climbwell.'
May these names in the future bring you good fortune, as a reward for your kindness to a poor old
woman."

Then she bade them good-by, reminded them once

more of their names, told them to act up to them, and turned away down the path.

In the evening, when their parents returned, the boys related what had occurred, and repeated the strange names they had been given. The old people were much astonished, and asked where the stranger had come from, and all particulars about her. But the boys could only tell what had happened, and the whole thing would soon have been forgotten, had it not been for the names. These they did not forget, and, strange to say, the more they were used the more the owner of each name seemed to develop the special quality that his name denoted, Watchwell, in addition, constituting himself the general guardian of the five. Was there a burden to carry, Holdwell's strong arms were ready. Did the parents require fagots for the winter, Hitwell could cut a pile, up in the dark pine woods on the mountains, that gladdened their hearts. Not a rabbit or bird could escape the keen eyes of Spywell, and by constant practise little Climbwell could scale the steepest cliffs along the fiord.

Years rolled on; the bright boys had grown up into tall, handsome young men, and all this time they had never crossed the high rocky hills that walled in their valley, never seen the great world that lay outside. But, now that they were men, a great wish was rising in their hearts to go forth from the old home and play their part among other men. The old people gave them their blessing, and bade them continue to stand by one another as they had ever done, for, if they only did that, there was nothing they could not achieve.

And so the young men departed, following the steep track over the high mountains at first, and then gradually leaving the hill country behind them as they went ever onwards. Sometimes they rested at a farmhouse, sometimes in a village, but nowhere did they find any permanent work. Many a farmer would gladly have engaged Watchwell and Spywell to guard his flocks, but he had no employment for Holdwell and Climbwell, and when the two last could have joined the village lads in fishing or seabird hunting, there was, again, no post for the other three. Still, they would not be discouraged. They had stout hearts and strong limbs, and the good fortune they sought must be found elsewhere. So on they went, climbing high mountains and fording swift rivers, till at last they entered an interminable dark pine wood with a tangled undergrowth of brambles and tall ferns. Hitwell cleared a path before them, and at length they emerged on a vast plain.

The sun was setting, and pouring a flood of crimson, gold, and purple over the scene before them.

The rays lit up the tall spires and high gray walls of a large city, and turned the broad, flowing river that encircled it into molten gold.

The brothers stood still entranced.

" It must be the city of the king," cried Watch-well, at length.

" Yes," said Spywell; " look, there is the royal flag flying on the tower of the palace."

They soon traversed the plain, and as darkness began to fall, they arrived at the great drawbridge over the river, and were directed to the palace by the warder. The king received them, and listened to their request for employment in his service. The brothers were such fine, handsome fellows that he was much taken with them as they stood before him. They were very tall, and had bright blue eyes, and fair curling hair. He told them that he could give employment to all five, if they would remain throughout the winter at his court, and watch and guard his daughters at the coming Christmas Eve.

" Do not, however, pledge yourselves to stay, until you learn the nature of the task that lies before you," he said. " For I have made a vow that the life of the next man who fails in this duty shall be forfeited. Perhaps you five brothers acting together can be more careful than strangers. Now listen.

Two years ago," he went on, "I had five fair daughters, but, alas! the Christmas before last my golden-haired Elma disappeared mysteriously in the dead of night. Search was made in all directions; no trace of her could be found. Last Christmas Eve the princesses' apartments were carefully watched and guarded; no strangers were admitted, only old and faithful servants were near them. But when morning came, Irene, my second daughter, was nowhere to be found, nor was there any sign of her captors' footsteps near the window of the room where she slept. I have now made a vow, and I shall keep it; but I also offer a reward. He who defends them faithfully this year shall wed the next eldest princess who would without his care have disappeared, and he shall be to me as a son. It will be death or honor. Choose, young men, now, while you are still quite free."

"We will stay and guard the princesses," they cried with one voice. "It is a task that will call all our qualities into full play. No robber can escape the eyes of Spywell, Holdwell will act up to his name, till Climbwell and Hitwell reach him, and I," and Watchwell drew himself up proudly, " *I* will be the one to forfeit my life if we fail."

So they remained at the court, and became great favorites with the king, who began to feel almost sorry that he had imposed sentence of death on the man who should fail to defend his daughters. He, therefore, determined to do what he could to make them safe, and caused a great tower to be built on to the palace with thick walls and windows very high up, and here the princesses were to sleep on Christmas Eve.

And now the time drew near. As usual great festivities were held for several days. On the last night, when the dancing and merry-making were all over, the three princesses—Frida, Ida, and Meya—were led to the tower by the king, attended by their ladies. As they lay down on the big couch, covered with silken embroideries, he bade them a last good night, and charged the five brothers to guard them with their lives. Then he left the tower, double-locking the great iron door that led into the rest of the castle. All was still. The brothers lay down on a rough bench in the ante-chamber, but the door of the princesses' room was wide open, and a lamp was kept burning there.

It had been a long and tiring day, and the younger brothers were soon fast asleep. But Watchwell never closed an eye. Wrapped in his long cloak, he leant against the wall and watched.

The night drew on. But what was that? He thought he saw a dark shadow slowly approach the

window of the princesses' room. As he looked, a
monstrous hand opened the lattice, and stretched
out gropingly towards the couch on which the king's
daughters lay asleep.

Watchwell touched his brothers. In an instant

"A MONSTROUS HAND OPENED THE LATTICE."

Holdwell had grasped the mysterious hand so tightly
that the owner could not move it; and Hitwell, with
one blow of his sword, severed it from the wrist. A
terrible wild cry of pain and baffled anger filled the
air, and, looking forth, the brothers saw a fearful
giant striding rapidly away from the palace, and
shaking his remaining hand threateningly towards

the tower. The noise had aroused the king, who was quickly on the spot, while Watchwell and his brothers hurried after the monster. Faster and faster he went, seeing he was pursued, but, though he was speedily out of sight, Spywell's keen eye traced his footsteps all the way.

On, on, on, they went, till at last they came to the foot of a high mountain. Steep and precipitous before them the sides rose up—no foothold to be seen anywhere. Climbwell, however, never hesitated. He showed his brothers a strong silken cord that he always carried with him, then, making a bold spring to a tiny ledge he had noticed, he commenced to climb, never taking a false step, till he reached the summit in safety. Then, lowering the silken rope, he drew up his brothers one after the other.

When they reached the top they found an enormous cavern, and just inside the entrance sat a huge giantess, on a low stool, crying bitterly. The brothers asked what ailed her.

"What matters it to you?" she said, and cried more than ever. But at last she told them that the previous night her husband had lost one of his hands, and she feared he would die, he was in such terrible pain. Then they told her that they could heal her husband if she would let them in, but "no one," they

said, "must be there but ourselves; we must bind
all others lest they should find out the secret of our
healing power."

The giantess, who was quite as wicked as her
husband, and had hoped to entice these young men,
by her pretended grief, into the cavern, so as to
provide a dinner for herself and her husband, did
not at all like the suggestion of being bound. But
she thought, perhaps, they might be able to heal
her husband first, so she submitted for the moment,
comforting herself with the hope that she could
easily break the rope and set herself free when the
young men had cured her husband.

Holdwell bound her with Climbwell's strong silken
rope, and then they passed into the inner cavern.
The giant was lying on his couch, and gave a howl
of rage when he saw them. But, crippled by the
loss of his hand, he was no match for the young
men, who speedily put an end to him. Then they
also killed the wicked giantess, who had quite a heap
of human bones beside her, and proceeded to explore
the inner cavern. They thought it might, perhaps,
contain some hidden treasure. But nothing was to
to be found, and they were on the point of leaving,
when Spywell descried a small door cunningly let
into the rock. Speedily breaking it open, a subter-
ranean passage was seen, leading to another cavern,

and there they discovered the two lost princesses—Elma, very pale and emaciated; whilst Irene, who had not been imprisoned so long, was more rosy and not so thin. The giant had evidently intended securing all five princesses before eating them.

The king's daughters were greatly overjoyed when they saw their noble deliverers, and heard that they were prisoners no longer. They quickly departed, Spywell and Climbwell having discovered an easier road for them to return by.

They arrived at the palace as night was falling, and the joy of the king at having his five daughters united once more can well be imagined.

A great banquet was hastily prepared, and before the assembled nobles and guests he related the brave deeds of Watchwell and his brothers, and announced that he had decided to wed his five daughters to the five heroes. " It is but right and fitting that men such as these, brave, noble and true, should reign over this land when I am gone," he said, " and to whom could I more worthily entrust my dear daughters than to those who have saved their lives ? "

Never was there so magnificent a wedding-feast. It lasted a whole month, and the dresses of the five princesses were perfect marvels of gold and silver embroidery and precious stones. Then to each brother was appointed a position in the State which

would call his special quality into play. They lived
long and happily with their respective wives, greatly
beloved and honored by all, and when at length
the old king died, Watchwell succeeded to the
throne, and his wise and good reign, together with
his beautiful and beloved Queen Elma, is still spoken
of to this day.

HERMOD AND HADVOR.

In the days long ago, there lived a king and queen. They had an only child, called Hadvör, who was not only the heiress to the crown, but was also the most beautiful maiden ever seen.

Now, the king and queen, having no son of their own, had adopted the child of a friend. The boy was called Hermod ; he was about the same age as Hadvör, and equally well-skilled in all knowledge that pertains to a young prince.

The young people had played together ever since they could remember anything, and the friendship of their childhood only strengthened as they grew older, and they promised to continue true to one another, no matter what might happen.

When they were about eighteen years old, the good queen sickened, and, feeling that her end was drawing near, she called the king to her bedside.

" Dear husband," she said, " I feel I have not long to live. Pray, therefore, grant me the last request I shall ever make you. I know how lonely you will be without me, and I hope, therefore, that you will

marry again. But, if you do, let it be the good
queen of Hetland, who has lately lost her husband, and who, having no children, will love our
dear ones as if they were her own."

The king, overwhelmed with grief, promised to
do as she wished; and the queen died peacefully.

For some time the king could think of nothing
but the terrible loss he had sustained. At length,
however, wearying of his lonely life, he fitted out a
ship, and went to sea.

After sailing along for some days under brilliant
sunshine, one morning a thick fog arose. It grew
denser and darker, and the sailors could no longer
tell which way they were going, when the mist suddenly lifted, and they saw land before them.

The king ordered a boat to be lowered, and was
rowed ashore. He then got out alone, telling the
men to wait for him.

Going quietly along, he presently came to a wood,
and the sun being very hot and the king very tired,
he was glad to sit down and rest under the shade of
a big oak tree. He had not been long there, however, when he heard music in the distance, and,
following the sound, he presently came to a beautiful open glade, and there he saw three women. One
of them, clad in richly embroidered robes, was seated
on a golden stool. She held a harp in her hand and

had evidently been playing, but she looked sad and troubled. Beside her, seated on a lower stool, was a young girl, also handsomely dressed, though not so richly as the elder women, and behind them stood another girl, also good-looking, but very plainly dressed, with a green cloak thrown round her. She evidently was the servant of the other two.

After gazing at the women for a few moments, the king stepped forward and saluted them respectfully.

The lady seated on the golden stool, having returned his greeting, asked him who he was and where he was going.

"Alas!" said the king, " I have lost my dear queen, and now, in accordance with her last wish, I am on my way to Hetland, to ask the widowed queen of that country to become my wife."

"Oh, king!" replied the lady. "How wonderful is the hand of fate! I am the queen you are in search of! Hetland has been overrun by Vikings, who burned and destroyed everything they did not carry off, and it was only by a miracle that I managed to escape with my daughter and my attendant here."

When the king heard this, he hesitated no longer, but at once offered to take her back as his bride.

After a slight hesitation, the lady accepted the

king's offer, and, having rested a little longer, the
king led the way back to the boat. They quickly
embarked, and, without any further adventures, arrived at the king's country, where a great wedding-
feast was immediately prepared, and the marriage
took place, amid great rejoicing.

For some little time matters went very smoothly.
Hermod and Hadvör kept much to themselves, leaving the queen and her daughter to enjoy all the
splendor and gaiety of the court. But, as the time
went on, Hadvör, who was always kind to those
about her, seeing that Olöf, the queen's attendant,
was much neglected and snubbed by her mistress,
took compassion on her, and often asked Olöf to
come and see her.

After some months a war broke out with one of
the neighboring countries, and the king had to go
forth at the head of his army. No sooner had he
sailed than the queen went to Hermod and told him
she wished him to marry her daughter.

"That I cannot do," replied Hermod, "for I love
Hadvör, and she alone shall be my wife."

Then the queen, finding that no persuasion and no
threats had any effect, got very angry.

"If you will not marry my daughter," she cried
angrily, "neither shall you wed Hadvör. I have not
forgotten the magic taught me by my mother, and,

as you will not obey me, I lay my spell on you. You shall live on a desert island, and all day long you shall roam about in the shape of a lion; only after sunset shall you return to your human form, and then you shall think of Hadvör and remember your former life, and thus suffer doubly in looking back on the past; and you shall not be freed from this enchantment till Hadvör succeeds in burning your lion's skin."

" I am in your power now," replied Hermod; but your punishment will overtake you ere long, for I also possess some magic gifts; and, though I am at present powerless, as soon as your wicked spell is broken, which it assuredly will be, you and your daughter, who is as wicked as you are, shall be turned into a rat and a mouse, and you will bite and tear each other till you kill one another."

So Hermod suddenly disappeared, and no one knew what had become of him. The queen made a pretense of sending out people to search for him, but no trace of him was found.

When Olöf next visited Hadvör, she found her in great grief at Hermod's disappearance.

" Nay, do not weep," she said; " the queen, by her wicked enchantments, has caused him to disappear for a time. Both she and her daughter are two wicked giantesses, who have only assumed their pres-

ent form, and when Hermod refused to marry her
daughter, she put in practise her magic arts. She
has transported him to a desert island, where he
will be a lion during the day, but resume his own
form every evening, and this charm will last until
you succeed in burning the lion's skin. The queen
has also further arranged that you are to marry her
brother, a terrible, three-headed giant, who lives
underground. I, too, have suffered from her arts,"
concluded Olöf; "she carried me away from my
parents' house, forcing me to serve her. Fortunately,
however, she is powerless to hurt me, for the green
cloak I always wear over my dress was a gift from
my godmother, and nothing can harm me while I
have it on."

Poor Hadvör! She felt very hopeless when she
heard of all her stepmother's wicked plots against
her, and entreated Olöf, by the love they bore each
other, to assist her.

This Olöf gladly promised she would do.

"But first, you must keep watch and guard against
the queen's brother," she said. "He lives in a cave
beneath the castle, and will rise beneath your
chamber some night. You must, therefore, always
keep a large pot of boiling pitch ready, and as soon
as you hear a great rumbling noise, like an earthquake, and see the ground cracking, at once pour

the boiling pitch down the cracks, and this will kill the giant. It is the only thing that can hurt him."

About this time, the king returned home from the wars, and was greatly distressed at Hermod's disappearance. He made inquiries and sent out messengers in all directions, but no trace of him could be found, and the queen had to use all her arts to console the king under the loss of his adopted son.

Hadvör meanwhile remained quietly in her own house. Following Olöf's advice, she kept ready the boiling pitch for the giant, and had not long to wait. One night, shortly after the king's return, she was suddenly awakened by a loud rumbling noise; the ground began to shake and tremble; but Hadvör, having been fully prepared, was not frightened, and summoned her maidens to assist her. Then, as the noises grew louder, and several great cracks appeared in the floor, Hadvör and the girls poured the boiling pitch down the open seams. Then gradually the noises ceased, till everything was perfectly quiet again.

The next morning the queen rose up early, and as soon as she was dressed she hurried to Princess Hadvör's house. There, lying on the ground outside, she saw the dead body of her brother the giant.

"Oh," cried the queen angrily, "that must be

Hadvör's work! But the minx need not think she shall go unpunished, and upset all my schemes;" and bending over the body of the uncouth monster, she continued: "By my magic power, I will that your body shall be transformed into that of a beautiful prince, and that Hadvör shall be accused of causing your death."

With these words she placed her hand on the giant's body, and immediately it was changed into the likeness of a handsome prince.

The queen then returned to the palace, and, pretending to weep, she told the king that she feared his daughter was a very wicked girl, though she always seemed so good, for that her brother, a brave and handsome prince, had come to ask Hadvör's hand in marriage, who without any rhyme or reason had caused him to be killed, for she, the queen, had just seen his dead body lying outside the princess's house.

When the king heard this, he hastened to Hadvör's house, accompanied by the queen; and when he saw the dead body lying there, just as the queen had described, he was very angry. He said he could not have wished for a handsomer or nobler son-in-law, and that he would gladly have consented to the marriage.

Then the queen begged that she might be allowed

to choose Hadvör's punishment, and the king, greatly incensed with his daughter, gave his consent.

So the queen said it would only be a just punishment that Hadvör, who had killed her brother, should be buried alive in the same grave with him; and the king, though sorry for his daughter, having given his royal word, said the queen's wishes must be carried out.

Olöf meanwhile, who, unknown to the queen, had overheard all that passed, hastened away to tell Hadvör. When the princess heard what the queen intended doing, she was very frightened, but Olöf comforted her and promised to help her.

"And remember, if you wish to bring Hermod back again, you must not mind undergoing some pain and suffering for him."

Olöf then brought her a short cloak, which she told Hadvör she must wear over her dress when she went into the grave or burial mound. The giant, she said, would be a spirit after he was buried.

"He will then ask you to cut off and give him one of your hands," continued Olöf; "but you must not promise to do this until he has told you where Hermod is, and how you are to get to him. Then when you want to get out of the grave, he will let you mount on his shoulder; but beware how you trust him: he will only help you to put you off your guard, and will take hold of your cloak and drag you back. See, therefore, that it is only loosely tied, so that when once you have your foot on the outer edge the cloak alone will remain in his hands.

Meanwhile the grave was being prepared, and when all was ready the body of the supposed prince was laid in it, and Hadvör, who was not allowed to say a word in her own defense, was lowered in beside him, and the grave was walled up and closed.

And then all happened as Olöf foretold. The supposed prince became a spirit, but in his former giant form, and asked Hadvör if she would let him cut off one of her hands and her hair, saying, "Only a maiden's hand will open the grave, and a maiden's hair will Hermod save." But Hadvör refused unless he first told her where Hermod was, and how she could get to him.

Then the giant said that the queen had banished Hermod to a desert island, and described exactly where it was.

"But you will not be able to reach him unless you cut off your hand," said the giant. "Then you must cut off your hair and plait it together and make it into sandals, and with these you will be able to cross both sea and land.

Hadvör at once carried out the giant's instructions.

She cut off her beautiful long golden hair, and plaiting it together, made herself a pair of sandals. Then thinking only of Harmod, bravely held out her hand for the giant to cut off, and declared she was ready to go.

The giant said he would help her, that she must climb upon his shoulder and touch the roof with the hand he had cut off, when the top of the grave would open. So she followed his directions; and no sooner was the grave open than the giant stretched up his hand and caught hold of her cloak, to pull her back. But with one spring Hadvör was outside the grave, the cloak slipped from her shoulders, remaining in the giant's hands; and, without waiting to look round, she flew along the road he had told her of.

She ran on for some time without venturing to stop or look round, until at length she reached the seashore. There, far, far away in the distance, she saw a high rocky island. Her sandals, however, enabled her to cross the water easily; but when she reached the island the shore was so steep and rocky, she could find no way of getting into the interior. This was a terrible disappointment and tired and weary with all she had gone through, Hadvör sat down on a fallen piece of rock, and presently fell asleep. Then she dreamt that a big giantess came up to her and said, " I know that you are Hadvör, the king's daughter, and that you are in search of Hermod. He is on this island; but you will not find it easy to reach him, if left to yourself, for the cliffs are steep and dangerous, and, though you are brave and ready to face any danger for him, you will not be able to climb them. But I will help you. Go round the corner of the next cliff, and there you will find a stout rope fastened to the rocks. By its help you will be able to climb up and get into the island. But it is large and has many caves, and you might be a long time ere you find Hermod. I have, therefore, brought you this ball of ribbon; take hold of the loose end, and the ball will roll along and guide you in the right way. I also give you this girdle; fasten it round your waist, and as long as you wear it you will suffer neither hunger nor fatigue. But remember to keep silence while Hermod is still under the spell, and on no account must you speak until after you have burnt the lion's skin."

When Hadvör awoke, feeling quite strong and refreshed, she thought she had only had a very pleasant dream; but, looking round, she saw a ball of gaily colored ribbon and a beautiful silken girdle lying beside her. Putting the girdle round her waist, she tucked the ball inside of it, and, going round the next cliff, she saw a stout rope hanging down.

Then she knew that her dream was no ordinary one. She took hold of the rope, and began climbing the almost perpendicular rock. But it was a long and difficult task, for the rocks were high and steep, and the loss of her hand greatly impeded her progress. But whenever she lost heart, she thought of Hermod, and the knowledge that she was at last near him gave her fresh strength, till at length she reached the top.

She then placed the ball on the ground and followed its lead, till it stopped at the entrance to a cave.

Cautiously Hadvör peeped in, but she saw nothing except a miserable wooden pallet, so she crept under this and hid herself.

The hours seemed very long, as she lay there listening for every sound that might announce Hermod's approach ; then, just as the sun was setting, sending a bright crimson gleam into the cave, she heard a loud roar, accompanied by heavy footsteps, and presently a huge lion entered the cave.

Hadvör's heart leapt into her mouth, but she remembered that she must be silent if she wished to save him.

The lion then went towards the hearth, and giving himself a vigorous shake, the lion's skin fell off, and Hadvör saw that it was indeed Hermod.

He sat down on the bed (little thinking that Hadvör was hid underneath), and began talking aloud of his love for Hadvör, and his great grief at their separation, and his utter inability to help himself. "For, alas!" he concluded, "it is only by Hadvör's finding and burning my lion's skin that I can ever get back my human figure and power; and how is it possible she should ever find me here?"

Hadvör, when she heard these words, almost jumped out from beneath the bed, but she remembered in time that she must not speak until she had burnt the lion's skin. So, with a strong effort of her will, she kept perfectly still and silent till Hermod threw himself down on the bed.

As soon as she heard that he was fast asleep, she crept forth quietly, and, taking an armful of wood and a lighted brand from the hearth, she made up a big fire outside the cave, and burnt the lion's skin Hermod had thrown off. She then returned to the cave and wakened Hermod. What a glad and joyful meeting that was!

Hadvör told Hermod all that had occurred after his disappearance, and how, by Olöf's help, she had been enabled to find him.

"Oh, Hadvör," cried Hermod, "to think of all you have done and suffered for my sake! And, alas, that you should have lost your right hand! How

can I ever make up to you for all you have done?"
And gently taking the maimed arm, he pressed his
lips to the wrist, when lo, and behold, the hand was
restored, and not even a mark was visible to show
where it had been severed!

Then they began planning how best to return
home, and Hadvör told Hermod of her wonderful
dream and the gifts she had already received from
the giantess. "Surely," she added, "she must live
somewhere on this island, and might help us
again."

Hermod said he believed a giantess did live on
the island, and that she was called Allgood, but he
had never seen her, though she was supposed to
watch over people and help them. So they determined to try and find her, and they sallied forth.
After a long search, they came to a huge cavern,
inside of which sat the great giantess, surrounded
by her fifteen children! Then Hermod asked her
if she would help them to return to their home, telling her how they had been driven forth.

"It will not be easy," replied Allgood, "because
the giant who was buried with Hadvör will try and
throw all kinds of obstacles in your way. He has
been changed into a huge whale, and swims all round
this island, and he will certainly try all he can to
kill Hadvör ere she reaches her own country. But

I will lend you my ship, for though Hadvör's sandals would carry you across the water, they will not protect you from the giant. He may not know that you are in my ship; but if you see him swimming towards you, I fear your life may be in danger. Then call on me, and I will help you."

Hermod and Hadvör thanked the giantess warmly for her good advice and kind offer of help, and getting on board her ship, where they found food and everything they wanted, they left the island, happy and hopeful. But ere long they saw a huge whale swimming rapidly towards them. He spouted the water up, yards high, and lashed the sea with his tail as he came near the ship.

"Oh, Hermod," cried Hadvör, "that surely must be the wicked giant! Let us call on Allgood to help us!" And they both called loudly on the giantess for aid.

Immediately a still bigger whale than the first one appeared, followed by fifteen smaller ones. They swam swiftly towards the ship, and when they had completely surrounded it, they turned on the first whale. Then a terrific battle began. The water shot almost up to the clouds, the sea was lashed into such great waves, that it seemed as if the vessel must be swamped, and Hermod and Hadvör watched eagerly for the result. The fight lasted for some time; but when at length it was over, they saw that the sea for some distance was red with the blood of the dead whale. And then the big whale, followed by the fifteen smaller ones, swam back to the island, and Hermod and Hadvör reached their own land in safety.

Meanwhile, strange events had happened at the king's castle. The queen and her daughter had disappeared, and in their apartments a big rat and a mouse fought all day and night. In vain the servants tried to drive them away. Even if they ran off for a short time, they always came back again and disturbed the whole castle by their cries. Thus some time passed, and the king was once again plunged into grief, not only at the disappearance of the queen, but because these horrid animals left neither him nor his court any peace.

One evening, when they were all assembled in the great hall, very sad and silent, quick steps were heard approaching, and, to the surprise of every one, Hermod entered. As soon as the king saw him, he embraced him warmly, greeting him like one returned from the dead, and anxiously inquiring all that had happened to him. But before sitting down, Hermod said he must first go to the queen's apartment. There the rat and mouse were fighting and biting one another, uttering frightful cries; but,

drawing his sword, Hermod smote them both, when,
to the amazement of all, there lay two hideous giantesses dead on the ground.   The servants quickly

"THERE THE RAT AND MOUSE WERE FIGHTING AND BITING ONE ANOTHER."

carried them out into the great courtyard, where
they were thrown on a pile of wood and burnt.

Meanwhile, the king and Hermod, accompanied
by the whole court, returned to the hall, and then
Hermod related all his wonderful adventures, greatly
to the delight and amazement of the king and his

courtiers. And, while they were exclaiming at the wonders of his tale, Hadvör came in, accompanied by Olöf.

Then, indeed, there was general rejoicing, and the king at once acceded to Hermod's wish to become his son-in-law. There was no long delay over the wedding, and as the king was now growing old, he handed over the government of the country to Hermod, whose reign is still known as that of "the good king."

Hadvör, in the midst of her own happiness, did not forget Olöf and all the good services she had rendered her. She married one of the great nobles of the kingdom, who became King Hermod's right hand, and Hadvör and Olöf remained close friends all the days of their life, their friendship descending to their children and grandchildren.

INGEBJORG.

THERE once lived a king and queen who ought to have been as happy as the day is long, for they had a fine kingdom, a beautiful palace, plenty of horses and carriages; their treasure-room was filled with gold, silver, and precious stones, and no matter how much they took out of it, it always remained full.

Their people were quiet and industrious, and they had no cares or troubles; yet, notwithstanding all this, they grew daily more sad and sorrowful, for they had no children to inherit all the riches they owned.

One day the queen went out into the palace garden. It was a fine bright winter's morning. The snow lay hard and firm on the ground, and each tree and bush sparkled and glistened in the sunshine, just as if the jewels in the king's treasury had been scattered over them.

The queen, feeling tired, sat down on a stone bench beneath a huge oak tree, when suddenly a large white bird flew down from the tree. It brushed past so close to the queen's face, that the wing-feathers scratched her cheek, and a few drops of bright crimson blood fell on the snowy ground.

" Oh," cried the queen, " would that I might have a daughter who would be as beautiful as those crimson drops on the white glistening ground ! "

" You shall have your wish," sang the bird, as it flew away, its white wings shining in the sun like silver.

The queen had hardly recovered from her surprise than she heard a noise behind her, and, turning round, she beheld the old man Surtur, who lived in a little hut near the palace, and who was well known and dreaded as a wicked magician.

" Ay, you shall have your wish," he muttered, in a fierce, angry voice ; " but I too intend to have a say in the matter. A daughter shall indeed be born to you, but she shall cause you more sorrow than happiness, unless, indeed, she returns you good for evil." And he laughed wickedly, and disappeared.

When the queen heard these words she was greatly troubled, for she knew that Surtur was her enemy, and that he was powerful ; but as weeks and months passed and nothing happened, she forgot all about the old man's words, and when at length her little daughter was born, every one agreed that she was the most beautiful child ever seen. She was chris-

10

tened Ingebjorg, and grew up as good as she was
beautiful.

At first the queen could not do enough for the
child, and could hardly bear her out of her sight;

"'AY, YOU SHALL HAVE YOUR WISH,' HE MUTTERED."

but as she grew older, and when she saw how **fond**
the king was of Ingebjörg, and how every one
praised and admired her, she began to grow **jealous**,
and all her love seemed to turn to hatred.

When the king saw this, he thought it would be better to separate Ingebjörg from her mother, so he built her a separate house, and there she lived with her own attendants. But this only made the queen still more angry. At last she fell ill, and sent for her daughter, and when the girl came to her bedside she whispered something in her ear, and then sent her back to her own house again. But from that day a change came over Ingebjörg. She no longer laughed and danced as was her wont, but walked about the rooms alone, often weeping, and would never leave her house on any pretext whatsoever.

One day, when Ingebjörg, as usual, sat in her room, her work that she used to take such pleasure in lying idly on her lap, while the tears rolled slowly down her cheeks, she heard some one knocking at the door, and on opening it she saw a funny little old woman with a high peaked hat, who asked if she might come in and rest.

Ingebjörg listlessly said " Yes ; " and then the old woman began telling her some wonderful stories, and at last Ingebjörg got so interested that her tears stopped, and she looked quite bright and happy like her old self.

" And now," continued the old woman, " I want you to come out into the wood with me. It is a lovely day, and so beautiful and fresh in the shade of the trees."

Though at first Ingebjörg declared she did not care to go, she at last allowed herself to be persuaded, and soon they were wandering along on the soft mossy paths beneath the beautiful great tall-stemmed firs, graceful beeches, and feathery birch, till gradually the sad look disappeared from Ingebjörg's face, and she began to laugh and run like the happy girl she had once been.

"And now," said the little old woman, when, tired of walking, they had seated themselves on a mossy bank, "now tell me, Ingebjörg, why are you always so sad?"

At first the girl refused to speak, but the little old woman kept on asking, and she looked so kind and gentle that at length Ingebjörg, said her mother had told her that it had been foretold at her birth that she was to marry a terrible giant, and that she was to burn her father's castle and so cause his death.

"And oh," cried Ingebjörg, "I love him so dearly! He has always been so good and kind to me! Oh, let us hasten home. I quite forgot; I ought never to have left my house, and I never *will* go out again, and then I cannot possibly harm him, or marry that horrible giant." And the poor girl hurried home, sobbing and crying all the way.

"Nay, nay," said the little old woman, " comfort yourself, my child. I am your godmother, and there is no harm done, and I think we can find some way to avert these evils. It is all that wicked Surtur's doing. He wanted to marry your mother, and when she would have nothing to say to him and married your father, he vowed he would never rest till the king was dead and she was punished. So he got her maid to give her some drops made out of the dragon's tooth, which turned her love for you to hatred and jealousy. But he can only work so far. It remains for you, now that you are grown up, to undo the evil he has wrought by returning good for evil, for love can overcome all things. The king's palace I cannot save, for my power only extends over living things; but neither your father nor mother shall be hurt, and the treasure can also be saved. Neither need you fear the giant if you will do exactly as I bid you. Now you must first go and persuade your father to go out riding in the forest with all his attendants."

With a heart greatly relieved at her godmother's cheery words, Ingebjörg hastened to do her bidding.

"Dear father," she said, as she entered his presence, "the day is so fine and the woods are so beautiful, will you not go out for a ride in the woods and take the courtiers with you?"

And the king, pleased at seeing her look so bright

and happy, at once said he would go, and with all
his courtiers in attendance, started off for a great
hunting party in the forest.

As soon as they were well out of sight, Ingebjörg
sent the servants away on different errands, and
when the palace was quite empty, the little old dame
helped the princess to carry out all the treasure and
whatever else was of value in the castle, and then,
when they stood in the great empty hall, she told
Ingebjörg that she must now take down the big can
of oil from the mantelshelf. In so doing the girl's
foot slipped, and the oil ran over the hearth and into
the fire. In a few minutes the whole place was in a
blaze, the little old dame and Ingebjörg having just
time to escape.

" Thus," said the old woman, " one part of old Surtur's enchantment has been fulfilled, without harm
to any one, and the rest you must now carry out; "
so saying, she gave Ingebjörg a little silver ball.
" Now go to the forest, throw down this ball, and
follow its windings till it stops at a woodman's hut;
go in, but keep the door ajar, so that you can see
who comes in, and, whatever you do, remember
that *you* must see the owner of the hut before he
sees you. Remain there till I summon you; but
when in your dreams you hear me calling you, do
not lose an instant, but hasten to the palace, for your

mother will need you. Remember love is the great conqueror, and can overcome all evils."

Ingebjörg promised to do exactly as the old dame had told her. She threw down the silver ball and followed its course as it rolled along, till at last it stopped before a woodman's hut, and, going in, she hid behind the half-closed door, peeping curiously between the slit.

Presently she saw a huge giant coming towards the hut, carrying a dead bear across his shoulders which he had killed out hunting. He pushed open the door, and, as he threw down his burden, he beheld Ingebjörg; however, she had seen him first, and felt very frightened.

But though he looked terribly fierce, his voice was very soft and kind as he told her that she might remain with him, but that she would have to make the beds, cook the food, and sweep the floor—all which Ingebjörg promised to do. He then showed her a little inner chamber where he said she might sleep. "And, whatever noises you hear," he added, "don't come in here unless I call you."

And thus passed three days. The giant went out early every morning, and never returned till sunset; while Ingebjörg cooked the food, made the beds, and kept the little hut clean and tidy. Every night she heard frightful noises in the outer room, the walls of the hut shook, and the earth trembled, but as the giant never called her, she lay quietly in her bed, pulling the clothes over her ears to deaden the terrible noises. And then, as she fell asleep, each night she dreamed that, instead of the giant, a handsome young prince stood beside the hearth.

On the third evening, she had hardly fallen asleep when she fancied she heard some one calling her. Quickly jumping out of bed, she hastily threw on her clothes, cautiously opened the door, and, seeing the hut was empty, she ran as quickly as she could to the palace. She knew that her mother needed her.

There, in front of the chief entrance, she saw a wooden stake had been driven into the ground, to which the queen was tied, while the servants were piling fagots of wood round her; for the queen had been condemned to be burnt to death for having set the palace on fire during the king's absence and stolen all the treasure, though she in vain pleaded her innocence.

Pushing her way through the crowd, Ingebjörg threw herself down on her knees before her father.

"Oh, stop, stop!" she cried eagerly. "Dear father, my mother is not to blame. It was I who was forced to burn down the castle, in order to save your life, which was threatened by the wicked magician, Surtur, and the treasure also is safe."

When the king heard this, he at once ordered the queen to be released, who, freed from the wicked spells that Surtur had thrown over her, embraced her daughter with many loving words.

Surtur, hearing that his evil deeds were known to the king, tried to hide himself in the woods; but he was caught and brought back by the giant, who had also fallen under his enchantments. But Ingebjörg remembered her silver ball, and, throwing it towards the giant, he caught it, and as he did so he was immediately changed into the handsome young prince Ingebjörg had seen each night in her dreams.

But Surtur was not to escape. The king called his servants, who bound the magician with strong cords. He was condemned to death for all his wicked deeds, and was led forth into the desert, where he was torn to pieces by wild horses.

All the queen's old jealousy now died out forever. She loved Ingebjörg more fondly each day, and before long there was a great marriage-feast between the prince and Ingebjörg. They lived happily together all the days of their life, and on the death of the king and queen, Ingebjörg and her husband reigned in their stead, beloved by all their people.

HANS.

CHAPTER I.

HANS STARTS ON HIS TRAVELS.

Once upon a time, many, many years ago, there was an old man and his wife who lived in a little cottage beside a big wood. They had three sons, called Kurt, Conrad, and Hans.

The father was very proud of his two elder boys, who were great tall fellows, but he never troubled about Hans, the youngest son, who, poor boy, often fared rather badly, as he only got whatever his brothers did not care to keep. He was never allowed to join in their games, or trials of skill, in which the father trained his elder boys, but had to stop at home, doing the housework and helping his mother in the kitchen. She was, indeed, the only one who ever showed him any love or kindness.

Thus poor Hans was often very sad and lonely, and so, in order to while away the time and have some kind of companionship, he got a kitten from a neighbor, teaching it all kinds of tricks, and as the animal grew older it became so attached to Hans that it followed him about wherever he went.

So matters went on till all three brothers were grown up. Kurt and Conrad gave themselves great airs, for, being tall and robust and well skilled in all games of strength, they laid down the law whenever they appeared on the village green, and bragged so loudly that most people were afraid to contradict them, more especially as their father backed them up in everything. He thought they could do no wrong, whereas Hans was always wrong and of no use at all; he ought, in fact, to have been a girl, always pinned to his mother's apron-string.

And thus ignored by his father, and set aside by his brothers, there was only his mother to stand up for Hans, but she only loved him all the more, and he in return was devoted to her.

One day Kurt and Conrad came home from the village, where they had come off victors in every trial of strength on the green, and so proud were they of this success, that they begged their father to let them start on their travels, and go and visit the king whose kingdom lay on the opposite side of the great arm of the sea near which stood their hut.

At first the father did not like the idea of parting

with his sons; but when he looked at them, and saw
what great strong fellows they were, he felt convinced that they would certainly win riches and
renown; so he agreed to let them go, fully convinced
they would return both famous and wealthy.

Not long after this, the father heard in the village
that a big ship lay in the offing, so he told his wife
she must get new shoes for Kurt and Conrad, as
well as money for the journey, for he meant them
to go to the great kingdom across the water, where
they would be sure to win both fame and riches.

The old woman did her best to obey her husband's
behests. She took the great hanks of flax she had
spun during the winter, and having sold these in
the village, she bought new shoes for Kurt and
Conrad with some of the money, keeping the rest
for their journey.

But when Hans saw all these preparations going
on, he had no rest or peace, and a great longing
came over him to be allowed to go with his brothers.

Plucking up his courage, he went to his father,
and begged and entreated to be allowed to accompany Kurt and Conrad.

At first the old man was very irate at what he
considered Hans' impertinence, and angrily refused.
But when he came to think over it, he decided that
he would rather not have him at home alone, when

the others were away, so he told him he might go, but only on condition that he did not join his brothers. He must keep quite apart from them, so that they need not be ashamed before strangers of its being known that such a small, useless fellow was their brother.

Although this was not a very gracious permission, Hans was only too pleased to get leave of any sort, so he hastened to his mother and begged her to try and fit him out also, like his brothers.

Kurt and Conrad, hearing that Hans had likewise got permission to go, hastened their own preparations and started at once, as they did not want him to go with them : but he was so anxious to get away and helped his mother so effectually, that he was ready almost as soon as they were.

When he came to bid her farewell, she gave him a small purse with her savings in it, and then handed him her oven crutch.*

" Take this also, Hans," she said ; " you will find it very useful, for you can use it either as a walking-stick or a weapon of defense, if you are in danger, and you will never lose your way, so long as you have it in your possession."

Hans thanked her warmly, bade his father good-

* This is a small bar of iron, about the size of a walking-stick, with a cross-piece at one end, still in use in Iceland.

by, and with another loving farewell to his mother, went forth on his travels, his cat sitting gravely on his shoulder.

He hurried along as quickly as he could, hoping he would yet be in time to overtake his brothers, but when he got down to the shore there was no sign either of them or the ship, which had evidently sailed some time before.

Unwilling to lose any chance, Hans kept along the shore for some time, thinking that perhaps the vessel had gone into some of the " fiords " that surrounded the coast; but, seeing no sign of a sail, he at last left the beach as the sun was setting, and took a path leading up towards the hills.

His cat, who had sat on his shoulder all this time, now jumped to the ground, purring and arching his back as he trotted beside Hans. Suddenly, a huge bird came flying rapidly towards them. Hans at once saw that it was a dragon, so he took a firm grasp of his iron crutch, waited till the creature was within reach, then, throwing it, hit him so cleverly that he fell to the ground; whereupon the cat, making a spring, speedily put an end to the monster.

When Hans ran up, he saw that the bird held something white between its talons, and stooping down, perceived it was a little girl, who cried most piteously.

Hans tenderly lifted the little thing in his arms, and tried his best to quiet her. But it was not till the big cat came up purring and rubbing itself against

"HANS SAW AT ONCE THAT IT WAS A DRAGON."

the wee creature, that she ceased her sobbing and was comforted.

Hans was now somewhat at a loss as to what he had best do. Night was coming on; there was no house in sight, and no food at hand. But just as he was driven to his wits' ends, he saw a little old man

running towards him, puffing and panting.   As soon
as he came up to Hans, he thanked him warmly for
having rescued his child from the dragon.

He was a quaint-looking little man, almost a dwarf,
but when he took the child in his arms and began to
soothe and quiet it, his face was so kind and gentle,
that Hans, who had expected to pass the night out-
of-doors, gladly accepted his offer to go home with
him and stay the night.

They walked on a long way, pussy always trotting
by her young master's side, till at length they came
to a big stone or rock.

Here the dwarf paused, and, knocking three times,
the stone opened.   Then the dwarf bade Hans enter,
and, giving three taps, the stone again closed.

When Hans looked round, he was surprised to find
himself in a fine large room, fitted up with every
comfort ; great couches, spread with soft rugs, ran
along two sides ; in one corner was the hearth, on
which a bright fire was burning ; and on the other
side was a table with some chairs beside it, and
covered with various papers and quaint instruments.

The old man put the child into a pretty little cot,
and after he and Hans had partaken of some food,
he invited the latter to rest.

Hans, nothing loath, threw himself on one of the
couches, with his cat beside him, and thoroughly

tired out with all the excitement of his departure and the long distance he had walked, fell asleep almost as soon as his head rested on the pillow. But even in his sleep he heard the dwarf working at his papers during the greater part of the night.

Next morning, after they had breakfasted and Hans was ready to start forth on his travels, the dwarf again thanked him for his timely rescue.

"I can never be grateful enough to you for saving my child," he continued. "And now I am going to give you three things, which I hope will be useful to you, though nothing can ever cancel my debt to you."

"Indeed you owe me but small thanks," replied Hans, laughing; "it was really my cat who saved your child, by killing the dragon ere I came up to him."

But though Hans declared he wanted no payment, the dwarf would take no denial.

"You see this small stone," he said; it possesses the power of making whoever holds it in his hand invisible. This sword," he continued, drawing forth a tiny but exquisitely damascened sword, "is both sharp and strong, and though small enough to carry in your pocket, you have but to express the wish when you need to use it, and it will at once attain its full size and strength. And here," he added, " is

I

my third gift. It is, as you see, but a tiny little ship, like a child's toy, so small that you can easily carry it also in your pocket, and yet, whenever you desire, it will become as large as you may need it either to go on a river or across the sea, and it further possesses the property of being able to sail, no matter whether there is any wind or not."

It was in vain that Hans protested he had in no way earned such valuable gifts. The dwarf insisted; so Hans was fain to take the precious treasures, thanking him most warmly for his great kindness. He then bade him farewell, kissed the pretty child, who clung round his neck, and, taking up his iron crutch, shouldered his cat and departed.

CHAPTER II.

HIS WONDERFUL ADVENTURES, AND HOW HE RETURNED
GOOD FOR EVIL.

WHEN Hans got down to the shore again, he drew
forth the little ship from his pocket, and putting it
in the water, said—

" Ship, ship, grow larger."

Immediately the tiny boat expanded, and behold
a beautiful vessel lay there at anchor.

Hans got on board, and then, having said where he
wished to go, the vessel sailed merrily along towards
the kingdom on the opposite side of the big sea.

When they were halfway across, a violent thunder-
storm came on ; but though he noticed that the other
vessels near him were tossed about by the great
waves, his ship sailed straight on towards its destination, and never lay-to or swerved aside till it was
safely anchored in its destined port.

As soon as Hans landed, he said, " Ship, ship, grow
smaller ! " and immediately the great vessel grew
smaller and smaller, till it was like a tiny little model
which he could easily put into his pocket.

Making sure that he had both his other treasures safely stowed away, Hans, with his faithful cat mounted on his shoulder, made his way inland.

Presently he came to a small wood, and here, sitting down beneath a fine, big oak tree, near which ran a bright sparkling stream, he decided to remain for a short time, studying the people and their habits, ere he went on to the king's palace.

Thanks to his faithful cat, he never lacked food, for puss went out night and morning, always returning with a rabbit or a bird for her master's dinner and supper.

Meanwhile, Kurt and Conrad on their arrival had gone straight to the palace, and had asked the king's permission to remain the winter with him. Although he did not really require their services, the king, seeing what fine strong fellows they were, gladly consented. So they joined the royal household, and were soon known as the merriest among the party, often boasting of their great feats of strength and the valiant deeds they had done.

After some weeks, Hans too arrived at the palace. At first he kept somewhat in the background, where no one noticed him, but whence he was able to observe everything that went on.

Now, the king had no son, but an only daughter named Gerda, who was both beautiful and wise.

The king, who was getting old, was anxious to see her happily married; but, although he had received numerous offers for her hand from neighboring princes and other strangers who had heard of the princess's beauty and wit, she had refused them all, for Gerda was difficult to please.

At length one day, just at the commencement of winter, and when all the foreign princes and courtiers were assembled in the big hall of the palace, the king announced that he had quite made up his mind to give his daughter, together with the half of his kingdom during his lifetime, to whomsoever would bring him by Christmas Eve, the three most precious treasures in his kingdom.

These were, a chess-board and men, made of pure gold and silver; a gold-handled sword, set with precious stones, in a golden scabbard, and with an unbreakable blade, and which always killed your enemy; and a wonderful bird with golden plumage, which, when it sang, could be heard in every part of the kingdom, yet its wondrous melodies were so sweet and soft, that they were not too loud even when quite near.

These marvelous treasures, said the king, had originally belonged to his ancestors; but, during a great war with the giants, many years ago, they had been carried off, and were now in possession of a terrible ogress, who lived on a rocky and almost inaccessible island, and always kept these treasures in a cave, on a shelf above her head, and they could only be taken away while the giantess was asleep.

The courtiers did not pay much attention to the king's words. They had heard them before, and they also knew that all those who had ventured on this quest, had either never been heard of again, or, if they returned, were maimed both in body and mind.

Some of the foreign princes, however, started off, hoping they might succeed. But when days elapsed and they did not return, Kurt and Conrad thought they would like to try. Knowing how big and strong they were, the task did not seem an impossible one to them, and they were eager to make the venture.

Kurt, therefore, as the eldest, came first before the king, and said that if he could have a ship and crew, he would gladly start in search of the treasures.

The king at once acceded to his request, a vessel was fitted out, and Kurt sailed away.

After many days, he at length reached the island, but, being still daylight when they arrived, they kept well out of sight, and did not attempt to land till it was dusk, when Kurt hoped the giantess might be asleep.

Then, making his way cautiously to the cave where

she lived, he peeped in, and there, sure enough, lay
the great ogress, fast asleep on her bed.

Creeping cautiously along the floor, Kurt looked
up for the shelf, and there he saw the three golden
treasures.

He hardly knew which to take first, so he decided
to begin with the most difficult one, and, cautiously
stretching forth his hand, laid hold of the bird,
which sat on its perch with its head tucked under
its wing, thinking to put it in his pocket. But unfortunately, he grasped it too roughly, and immediately the bird began to screech so loudly, that
the whole cave shook and trembled.

In an instant the giantess sprang from her bed,
caught hold of Kurt, threw him down on the ground,
and tied his hands and feet firmly with ropes.

" Ha ! ha ! " she laughed. " Here is another one !
What fools they all are, to think they could outwit
me ! But this one will do nicely for my Christmas
dinner when I have fed him up a little." And with
these words, and despite his loud cries and remon-
strances, she trundled him into a small cave at the
back. " And you need not fear that I shall starve
you," she grinned maliciously, "for I want you to
get nice and fat ; at present you are so thin, you are
not worth eating." So saying, she ran out of the
cave and hurried down to the shore, hoping to catch

some of the crew, and so fill her larder still further.

But no sooner did the men see the monster running down to the shore, than they rowed back to the ship with all their might, and, lifting the anchor, set sail at once, and were soon out of sight.

When the men returned home and described the awful ogress who had raced down to the shore to catch them, the king feared there was but little hope that Kurt would ever be heard of again.

But after a few days, Conrad began to think that if *he* had gone, he would have managed more cleverly than Kurt, so he asked the king if he would fit out a ship for him and let him try his luck.

The king, anxious to recover his treasures, at once agreed ; and full of hope, feeling quite sure his skill and cleverness would not fail him, Conrad started on his journey.

But, alas ! he was no more lucky than his elder brother. When he got to the cave, he also found the giantess asleep, and, after considering which of the three treasures he should take first, he decided for the sword.

"The bird may make a noise if it sees me," he thought, "whereas if I have the sword, should the giantess awake, I will kill her, and then secure all three treasures."

So he watched for a few minutes to make quite sure that both the giantess and the bird were asleep, then stealing cautiously on tiptoe across the floor of the cave, he reached up to the shelf and stretched his hand out to take the sword. But, alas! in his eagerness he only grasped the handle of the weapon, and with a loud crash the scabbard fell down.

The bird began to scream, and in an instant the giantess sprang from her bed and had Conrad down on the floor, where she at once tied him up with ropes, as she had his brother.

"Ha, ha!" she croaked. "Here is another one! Oh, these fools, these fools! But if they will only come on fast enough, I need not stint myself, for I shall have a well-stocked larder by Christmas time?"

And ere he knew what was to happen to him, Conrad found himself inside the small cave beside his brother Kurt.

"Don't be afraid that I shall starve you," laughed the ogress; "you shall have plenty of food, and you must eat all you can, and get fat as quickly as possible, and then I shall release you;" and she grinned and laughed so loudly, that the whole cave shook and trembled as if there had been an earthquake.

Soon after the second vessel had returned to the court, the men giving the same account of what had

occurred as those in the first vessel, Hans suddenly
disappeared. He had become such a great favorite
at court, that every one was very sorry when he
thus suddenly vanished.

But he too was determined to try his luck, and see
if he could not carry off the treasures, and so win
the beautiful Princess Gerda, who had been most
kind to him during his stay at her father's court.

So one evening, just as the sun was setting, he
walked quietly down to the shore, Puss as usual
sitting on his shoulder, and, having placed his little
ship in the water, and pronounced the magic words,
he arrived at the giantess's island about the middle
of the day.

Having landed, Hans took his stone out of his
pocket, and thus at once becoming invisible, started
off for the ogress's cave.

Looking in, he saw it was empty, so, although he
was invisible, he thought it better to hide behind a
projecting bit of rock, in case she might knock up
against him.

As evening closed in, the giantess returned. But
no sooner had she entered the cave, than she sniffed
about in all directions—

"Phew! it smells of humans here!" she muttered.
Not seeing any one, however, she concluded it must
be the two men she was fattening up in the inner

cave. So, after a little time, she lay down on her bed. For some time she could not sleep, and kept on muttering, "Phew! It is very strange that I should smell those humans so strongly to-night! I could have sworn there was a fresh human here!"

At last, after tossing about restlessly, she dropped off asleep.

Hans crept forth softly, but the fire on the hearth had died so low, he could not well see his way, and stumbled over a small stone. In an instant the golden bird raised its head, but just as it was going to give a shrill scream, Hans's big cat pounced on it and silenced it.

Then the giantess started up, and, jumping out of bed, began feeling all round the walls, swearing angrily.

Hans knew that he must kill her, for, though he was invisible, if she caught hold of him she would certainly kill him. He therefore drew the sword which the dwarf had given him, out of his pocket and wished it to grow bigger. Then, when the giantess came near him, and stretched out her huge arms to throw him down, Hans, with one blow of his sword, cut off her head, which rolled away into a corner.

Hans then blew up the fire, and began searching round the cave; in addition to the king's three treasures, he found several great chests filled with gold and precious stones. Then he noticed that there was a smaller cave at the back, and, lighting a pine knot, he entered and found his brothers. He immediately loosened their bands, and they were both so grateful to be freed from the terrible fate in store for them that they ever after treated him as true brothers should.

They all three then set to work and carried the treasures from the cave to the ship, and when everything had been taken on board they quickly returned to the king's country, where they arrived on Christmas Eve, greatly to the astonishment of the whole court, who had quite given them up as lost.

But greater still was the surprise of every one, when Hans presented the king with the three treasures which had been so long lost, and were now once again restored to the kingdom.

The king was so delighted at having at last gained his wish, and recovered the long-lost treasures, that he told Hans he should always look upon him as a dear son, and that he should certainly marry his daughter.

So Hans was dressed in royal robes, and very shortly after married the fair Princess Gerda, who had long secretly admired him. The wedding was held with all possible magnificence. No expense was spared, and gifts were given to all the poor in the land.

The king then divided his kingdom in half, putting Hans in charge of one; whereupon, he sent for his father and mother, and gave them a good house and sufficient money to live in comfort for the rest of their days. And the two elder brothers were also provided for.

Hans and Gerda reigned long and happily. Puss always had a place of honor beside his beloved master, and lived long enough to see Hans's children and even grandchildren.

THE GIANTESS AND THE GRANITE BOAT.

Once upon a time there lived a king and queen who were greatly beloved by all their people. They had only one son, named Sigurd, who, even as a boy, was distinguished for his marvelous skill and dexterity in all manly sports and pastimes, whilst his strength was only equaled by his wisdom and his handsome person.

Years passed on. Sigurd had become a man, when one day the king called him to him.

"My son," he said, "it is now time for you to choose a fitting bride. I am getting old, and cannot expect to live much longer. You must take my place in a few years, and must try to gain men's respect and esteem by showing yourself capable of winning a princess worthy to share your throne. Visit first the country of Hardrada, my friend. His daughter is indeed, I hear, a marvel of beauty and goodness."

Sigurd at once prepared to start on his journey. With a few chosen companions, he set sail in his

174

noble galley, the high prow breasting the waves, and the stern, all gorgeous with carving and gilding, glittering in the sun. After sailing for some days over the tossing waters, the vessel at length reached Hardrada's country. It was night, one of those glorious summer nights of the north, when the moon is almost as brilliant as the sun. The bold shore, with its strange, grotesque crags and peaks, seemed utterly unapproachable, till suddenly a large creek or fiord was seen, at the head of which rose the king's palace. The windows were all ablaze with light, and the sounds of music and revelry told the travelers that some banquet was in progress.

Leaving their ship, Sigurd and his companions proceeded towards the palace, where they received the warmest of welcomes from the king and his daughter Helga. The princess was indeed all she had been pictured, tall and beautiful, and so gentle and charming that Sigurd made up his mind to win her. Next morning he acquainted the king with the object of his journey, and gained his consent. Hardrada was indeed anxious to have a son-in-law to share the cares of his kingdom, which, now that he was an old man, weighed heavily upon him. As a condition of his remaining with Hardrada, Sigurd only stipulated that he should return to his own country directly his father sent for him.

So the marriage of Sigurd the brave with Helga the fair took place with great pomp and rejoicing, Thanes and nobles coming from all parts to bring presents to the young people.

Sigurd and his wife loved each other very dearly, and their happiness was completed when, after the lapse of a year, a son was born to them, inheriting the beauty of the mother, and the strength and handsome form of the father. Three happy years thus passed away, little Kurt being two years old, when Sigurd received the news of his father's death and a recall to his native land.

It was a sad parting between Helga and her father; but Sigurd dared not linger, and once more the beautiful Viking ship started on its voyage through the sun-tipped waves, bearing the young king and his wife and child.

For several days the wind was favorable; but when within a day's sail of Sigurd's country the vessel ran into an extraordinary calm. Day after day the sun blazed down fierce and strong; not a breath of air was to be felt. In the forepart of the vessel, the men had all gone below. Sigurd's companions were also asleep, while he and his wife remained on deck, beneath the awning, talking quietly, with little Kurt playing at their feet. After a little, a strange drowsiness seemed to overpower Sigurd himself, and, declaring he could no longer keep awake, he too went below, and fell asleep like the others.

Helga was now quite alone on deck with her boy. Suddenly, as she was playing with him, she saw a strange object moving slowly along the smooth surface of the water. Shading her eyes with her hands, she watched it, and as it came nearer she made out that it was a boat, with a curious, ungainly form seated in it rowing.

Nearer and nearer it came, with silent, swift strokes, and as it touched the vessel with a hard sound the queen saw that it was very large and cut out of granite. With one spring the terrible giantess who had been rowing it was on deck. Like one in a dream, the queen could neither move nor utter a sound to arouse the king or the ship's crew. She seemed held by an invisible power. The giantess came up to her, and, snatching away the child, placed him behind her; then she proceeded to take off all the young queen's beautiful embroidered robes, leaving her only a single linen garment, and as she herself put on Helga's clothes, she gradually also assumed her shape and likeness. Lastly, she seized the queen and placed her in the granite boat, saying as she did so, in a terrible voice—

"Obey my words and my magic spell. Thou
12

must neither rest nor pause on the way, till thou
reachest my brother in the lower regions."

The poor queen, half fainting and utterly powerless, sat still and silent in the boat like a statue.
With a strong push the giantess sent the boat from
the vessel's side, and it was speedily lost to sight.
Then little Kurt began to cry. In vain the giantess
tried to soothe him; the more she attempted it the
worse he became, till at length, losing all patience,
she snatched him up and carried him down to the
king.

Waking him roughly, she upbraided him loudly
for leaving her alone on deck with the child.

"It was most careless and negligent of you," she
went on. "Some one ought to have been left on
guard while you were asleep. No one can tell what
may happen when one is thus left alone. As it is, I
found it impossible to quiet the child; I have therefore brought him down here, which is the proper
place for him. It is high time you roused your lazy
crew. A favorable wind has at last sprung up, and
we can have a chance of getting off this wretched
ship."

Sigurd was astonished at being addressed by his
queen in such terms. In all their married life he
had never heard her speak like that. He, however,
decided to take no notice of it; she must be over-

tired with the heat, he thought, and, answering her very gently, he endeavored to quiet the child. The little fellow, however, sobbed and cried as much as ever.

By this time the crew were aroused, the sails hoisted, and, the wind freshening splendidly, they reached land the following day. Here the whole country was still in mourning for the late king. But the people rejoiced greatly when it became known that Sigurd had returned in safety. He was crowned amid universal acclamations, and at once took the reins of government into his hands.

But ever since the strange calm at sea the king's little son had never ceased crying and sobbing, especially in the presence of his supposed mother, while before that time he had been a remarkably happy, affectionate child. The king, therefore, chose a nurse for him from among the people at his court, and when he was with her the little fellow seemed to be once more the bright, happy child he had been.

The king could not, however, understand the change that had come over the queen ever since their journey. She who formerly had always been so good and gentle, was now obstinate, cross, and untruthful. And ere long others began to notice the disagreeable, quarrelsome nature of the king's wife.

Now, there were at the court two young men who were so devoted to playing chess that they would sit for hours over their game, instead of joining in the outdoor sports of the other young courtiers. As they were the king's cousins, their room was in the palace, and it happened to be next to that of the queen. She had been particularly rude and disagreeable to them ever since she came, and they would have been glad to revenge themselves upon her in any way.

One day, hearing her moving about and talking angrily, they looked through a slit in the door, and distinctly heard her say—

"When I yawn slightly, I grow small and dainty, like a young maiden; when I give a bigger yawn, I grow into half a giantess; but when I stretch out my arms and yawn with all my might, I return to my original size, and become a mighty giantess."

And as she said these words, she stretched herself, yawned frightfully, as if her jaws would break, and suddenly grew into a monstrous and terrible giantess. Then, stamping her foot, the floor opened, and up came a three-headed giant, bearing a huge trough of raw meat. Greeting the queen as his sister, he placed the trough before her, and she devoured the contents, never resting till she had emptied it.

The two young courtiers watched this strange

scene, though they could not hear all that the giantess and her brother said to one another. They were horrified to see how greedily she devoured the raw meat, and amazed at the quantity she ate, for at the king's table she only picked daintily at the dishes. As soon as she had emptied the trough, the three-headed giant disappeared in the same manner as he had come, and the queen, giving a slight yawn, at once assumed her human figure again. The young princes then returned to their game, discussing the mystery in undertones.

And what of the king's little son all this time. One evening, when the nurse had lighted her lamp and was playing with the child in her arms, some of the boards in the center of the floor opened, and a most lovely lady, wearing only a single white linen garment, stepped forth. Her waist was encircled by a heavy iron ring, to which was attached a chain, which descended right down through the hole in the floor.

With a soft little cry, she ran up to the nurse, took the little boy in her arms, kissed him and fondled him, and, after lavishing no end of caresses on him, gently placed him back in his nurse's arms and disappeared in the same way as she had come, the floor closing over her again. All this time she never spoke a single word.

The nurse was greatly amazed at the incident, but, startled though she was, she did not say a word to any one. The next evening the same thing occurred. The white-robed lady came up through the floor, took the child, kissed and caressed him lovingly, and then replaced him in his nurse's arms. But this time, when she prepared to descend, she murmured, in sorrowful tones, "Twice this happiness has been permitted. Once more, and then all will be over."

Then she disappeared, and the floor closed over her as before.

The nurse became greatly alarmed when she heard the white lady say those words. She feared that some danger must threaten the child, and yet she had been much taken with the stranger, who had caressed the boy as if he were her own. She therefore thought it best to speak to the king, tell him what had happened, and beg him to be present at the time when the white-robed lady was wont to appear. The king listened attentively to the woman's story, and, suspecting foul play, promised he would be there.

The following evening, therefore, found him betimes in the nursery, seated in a chair, with his sword drawn, close to the spot where the stranger had always appeared. He had not long to wait.

"FORTH STEPPED THE BEAUTIFUL WHITE-ROBED FIGURE."
Page 188.

Icelandic Fairy Tales.

With a faint grating noise the boards opened, and forth stepped the beautiful white-robed figure, with the iron ring round her waist, and the long trailing chain.

In an instant Sigurd recognized in her his own beloved wife, Helga, and quick as lightning he seized her in his arms, and with one stroke of his sword cut the chain that fastened her. Immediately the most terrible groans and rumblings issued from the earth, the whole castle rocked and trembled, and every one thought that an earthquake was taking place. But in a short time the unearthly sounds ceased without any damage having been done.

Then Helga related to her dear lord all that had befallen her—how the wicked giantess had come to the ship in her granite boat when they were all asleep, and with her magic power had taken away all her clothes and put them on herself.

" When she had placed me in the granite boat, it floated on by itself, until the ship was quite out of sight," she continued, " and then I perceived we were going towards a large dark object, which, as we came near to land, I saw was a huge three-headed giant. He wanted me to marry him, but I steadfastly refused to be his wife, whereupon he chained me up in a big lonely cave, telling me I should never be free unless I consented. Every second day he came, repeating the same request and the same threats. Then, as time went on and I saw no hope of help, I began to think how I could escape his hands. At last I told him that I would be his wife if he would allow me to visit my son on the earth for three days running. At first he would not consent, but when I persisted he gave in ; but I had to promise that I would not say who I was. He then placed this iron ring round my waist, to which he attached a chain, the other end being fastened to himself. I hoped that perhaps one evening you might be there when I came to see our little Kurt. How sadly my heart failed me when the second evening passed without my seeing you ! But my prayers never ceased, and now my reward has come. The terrible groans when you cut the chain must have been the giant. He would fall when the strain was suddenly taken off the chain, for he lives right under the castle. He probably broke his neck when he fell, and the terrible shock must have been his death-throes."

Now the king saw clearly why he could not reconcile the behavior of the giantess with that of the gentle Helga, his own dear queen. The hideous impostor, who had now reverted to her original form, was summoned before the State Council, and, as additional evidence against her, the two young princes related what they had heard and seen. She was condemned to be stoned to death, and her body was put into a sack and torn to pieces by wild horses.

Then the real queen was invested with all her rightful honors, and soon won the hearts of her people. And little Kurt's nurse was not forgotten. She was married to a great nobleman, the king and queen giving her a rich dowry. She and her husband remained to the end of their days the friends of Sigurd and Helga.

GREYBEARD.

CHAPTER I.

THE STRANGE ADVENTURES OF GEIR.

ONCE upon a time, there lived a king and queen in a magnificent palace, surrounded by lovely gardens. Beyond them there stretched out great fields and meadows, in which grazed large flocks of sheep and herds of cattle, all of which belonged to the king, and beyond these again there was a beautiful big forest. But in addition to all this, they had an only child called Sigrid, who was known as the fairest princess in all the land.

Now, the king of one of the neighboring kingdoms wanted to marry the princess, and as he was very rich, her father and mother thought they could not do better than give him their daughter.

But Sigrid much preferred her young cousin Olaf, who, having lost his parents when a child, had been brought up with her, and who was as brave and handsome as the king (her suitor) was old and ugly.

186

When her father and the queen found that the princess would have nothing to say to the old king, they determined to send Olaf away.

" But we must be careful how we do it, and pretend it is for his good," said the queen ; " for remember, he has a fairy godmother."

So the king sent for Olaf his nephew, and told him he wished him to travel for a year and see something of the world.

" For it is not a good thing," said he, " for a young man always to stay at home. Go, therefore, to all the neighboring kingdoms, and see what is done in other lands."

The parting between Olaf and Sigrid was very sad, for he feared that the king and queen would force her to marry the rich old king during his absence, and Sigrid dreaded the dangers that might befall Olaf during his travels. But they promised to remain true to one another, and that nothing but death should part them. And then Olaf started on his journey.

Now, on the borders of the king's forest there lived an old man and his wife. The old man was called Geir, and his wife Trude. The old couple were very, very poor ; their little hut contained only the barest necessaries, but they had one cow, and having no children, the old man and his wife managed to live on the milk from their cow, and on the roots they gathered in the king's forest.

One Sunday, Trude, feeling very tired, said she would stay at home and rest, while her husband went alone to the village church. The pastor's sermon that Sunday was on charity, and Geir returned home greatly delighted with what he had heard. In the evening, as they were sitting beside the hearth, his wife asked him what the sermon had been about.

"Oh," said Geir, "it was the best sermon I have ever heard. The pastor said that, whoever gave away what he possessed, it would be returned to him an hundredfold, and I mean to try it."

"Ah," said his wife, shaking her head, "I don't think he can quite have meant that. You must have misunderstood him."

But Geir maintained that he was right, and so they went on disputing for more than an hour without either convincing the other.

The next morning, the old man hastened into the forest, and getting together a lot of woodcutters, he persuaded them to help him to build a hundred stalls. His wife grew very angry, and scolded him well for his folly, as she called it; but he turned a deaf ear to all her remonstrance, and continued his work. When the stalls were ready, Geir sat down and began to think who would be the best person to give his cow to, and so get a hundred cows in return.

" Surely, there is no one so rich as the king," soliloquized Geir; " he could easily give me a hundred cows for my one cow." And thus thinking, he led forth his cow, despite all the angry protestations of his wife.

When he had gone about halfway, a tremendous storm arose. Heavy black clouds rolled up from the north, the lightning flashed, and he could hardly stand up under the drenching showers of rain and hail, whilst the cow, terrified at the noise and darkness, struggled frantically to get away.

" Alas," sighed the old man, " I fear I shall have to let her go, for I cannot hold on much longer. It is so dark, I cannot see a step before me, nor do I know in which direction to travel! Alas, alas! it will be a wonder if I ever reach home alive! "

While he was thus wandering helplessly about in the dark, bewailing himself, and not knowing which way to turn, he suddenly saw an old woman standing before him, with a large sack on her shoulders.

" What are you doing out in such weather with your cow ? " she asked.

Then Geir told her why he had set forth with his cow, and what a rich return he hoped to get.

" You will certainly lose your own cow, in place of

getting a hundred new ones, and probably lose your own life too," said the old woman. "You had much better give me your cow, which is leading you a fine dance, and take this sack in exchange. See, you can easily carry it on your back, and I promise you you will find it contains good flesh and bones."

At first Geir would not hear of the exchange; but finding the animal grow more and more restive and wild, he at last consented, and no sooner had the old woman got the cow, than both she and it disappeared.

After some difficulty, the old man managed to lift the sack on to his shoulders, and, the storm having exhausted itself, made the best of his way home, groaning and panting under his burden, which seemed to grow heavier and heavier as he went on.

At length he reached his hut, and told his wife what had happened to him, making a great to do over the sack he had carried, and all the good food it contained.

"Oh dear, oh dear!" cried Trude, wringing her hands. "I do think you grow more stupid every day! It was bad enough to take away our only cow, and now you come back bringing an old sack!"

But Geir told her not to scold. She had better fill the big pot with water and put it on the fire, for had not the old woman told him the sack contained good flesh and bones?

Trude did as she was told, though grumbling the while, and when the pot began to boil, Geir went to the sack to untie it. But, behold, no sooner did he touch the string than the sack began to move and twist and turn about.

"There is something alive inside," cried Trude, terrified; "open it quickly." And when Geir had untied the string, out stepped a little man dressed from head to foot in gray; even his hair and beard were gray.

"If you want to cook anything for your supper," he cried laughingly, "I hope you will try your hand on something else than me."

Poor Geir was struck dumb with amazement; but his wife made up for his silence, and jeered and laughed at him for his folly and stupidity.

"First you get rid of our only means of support, and now, when we know not how or where to get food for ourselves, you bring home another mouth to feed, and so add to our burden. You surely must have lost the little wit you ever had!"

And thus the war of words raged till the man in gray said—

"Your wrangling will do none of us any good. Rather let me go out and see if I cannot bring back

some food for supper.   We shall certainly not grow
fat on your quarrels."

So saying, and without awaiting a reply, he opened
the door and sallied forth in the darkness, and ere
the old couple could come to any decision as to who
or what he was, good geni or wicked sprite, the
gray man returned, bringing back with him a nice
fat sheep ready killed.

"There," he said, throwing it down, "now you
can prepare some food, so that we may eat."

Geir scratched his head, and looked at Trude.
She returned the glance, and then they both looked
at the gray man.   Surely he must have stolen the
sheep!   They did not know what to do.

But at length hunger got the better of their
scruples, and, following the directions of Greybeard,
as they called him, they cut up the sheep, cooked a
portion of it for their supper, and lived in comfort
on the remainder for several days.   When that
sheep was finished, Greybeard brought in another,
then a third, then a fourth, and also a fifth.

By this time Greybeard had become a very
welcome guest, and the old people wondered how
they could ever have lived without him.

CHAPTER II.

HOW GREYBEARD OUTWITTED THE KING AND WON
PRINCESS SIGRID.

AND now we must take a peep at the king's
palace.

It was just a year since Prince Olaf had started
on his travels, and as nothing had been heard of him
from any of the knights or wandering minstrels
who traveled about from one country to another,
the king and queen told Sigrid that it was no use
waiting any longer, and that she must marry the
rich old king.

In vain she protested that she would rather not
marry at all if she could not wed Olaf. But the
king said that was all nonsense; princesses must
marry. And so the preparations for the wedding
were begun, for both the king and queen determined
that the marriage feast should be on a most magnificent scale. All the neighboring kings and
queens, and princes and princesses were invited, and
as the feasting was to continue for a whole week,
all the royal cooks and bakers were busy from morning till night.

16

Now, the royal shepherd had noticed that, for some time past, one of the sheep from his flocks disappeared every few days. He puzzled his head to try and find out the cause, but so far he had not succeeded, and when the fifth sheep disappeared he went to the king and told him what had happened.

"There surely must be a thief about the court," he added. "That is the only way I can account for the loss of the sheep."

On hearing this the king got very angry, and immediately made inquiries if any strangers had been seen in the neighborhood lately. At first he could learn nothing; but at last one of the servants said he had heard there was a little man dressed in gray whom no one knew, and who lived in the hut of old Geir and his wife.

Then the king sent messengers to the hut, commanding the immediate presence of the stranger in the great audience hall of the palace.

The old couple were greatly terrified when they heard this message. They made sure that their kind guest, through whose means they had been preserved from starvation, would be hanged as a thief. But Greybeard did not seem the least frightened, and prepared cheerfully to return with the king's messenger.

When he entered the great hall, the king asked

him if he was the man who had stolen the five sheep.

"Yes, sire," replied Greybeard; "I do not deny it."

"And pray, may I ask *why* you did it?" demanded the king.

"I did not go very far beyond my rights," replied Greybeard. "Besides, the old people who live in the hut yonder, are no longer able to support themselves," he continued; "they had no food, while you, oh, king, have plenty, and more than you can possibly use. It seemed only fair to me, therefore, that they should have as much as they needed, of that which you did not require, and could not use."

The king was at first inclined to be angry at this cool rejoinder; but he then became amused at Greybeard's coolness—it just reminded him of what Prince Olaf used to do. So he laughed, and asked him if the art of thieving was the only thing he had ever learned.

"No, sire," replied Greybeard, smiling; "I took no more than I had a fair right to, neither did I take it for myself, nor did I deprive you of anything you really needed."

"Well," said the king, "you certainly are a funny fellow, and always ready with an answer. But though I won't hang you for stealing my sheep, I must give you a lesson. To-morrow I will send my servants into the forest with my young red bull. If you succeed in stealing him, you shall be pardoned, but if you fail, you shall be hanged."

"I do not think I could steal the bull," replied Greybeard, "for, of course, you will have him carefully guarded."

"That is your affair," answered the king; "see that you do not fail."

When Greybeard returned to the hut, the old people received him with great joy, for they feared they should never see him again. He asked them if they had a stout rope, as he would need it next morning. Trude searched in her cupboards, and luckily found a nice bit of strong rope. This she gave Greybeard, and then all three retired to rest.

At break of day, Greybeard got up very quietly, dressed himself, and, taking the rope, left the hut.

He went to that part of the forest where he knew the king's servants must pass with the young bull. Climbing up into a big oak tree that stood close to the side of the road, he wound the rope round his body, and, crawling along a thick branch, he dropped gently from it, the rope under his arms, and his head hanging on his breast.

Presently he heard the king's servants coming along with the young bull. As they came near the tree, they looked up, and saw, as they thought, the gray man, hanging apparently lifeless from the branch.

"Aha!" said one, "no doubt he has been robbing others beside our king, and so they have hanged him! Serve him right, the rascal; he will not

"THE GRAY MAN, HANGING APPARENTLY LIFELESS FROM THE BRANCH."

trouble us again, or try to steal the bull!" So they passed on, quite satisfied that their enemy was dead.

But no sooner were they out of sight, than Greybeard climbed down, and taking a short cut through the brushwood, known only to himself, he was soon well in advance of the men. Quickly climbing up

another big oak that stood near the road by which
the king's servants had to pass, he again twisted
the rope round his body and hung down from the
branch.

When the men arrived with the bull, they were
greatly surprised to see another gray man hanging
from the tree.

" Could there possibly be two Greybeards?" they
asked each other, "or was there some magic at
work?"

"Listen," said the chief servant, "we will leave
the bull here, run back to the other tree, and find
out whether there are two Greybeards, or whether
the same man hangs from both trees."

So saying, they fastened the bull to the tree with
a stout rope, and ran back the way they had come.

No sooner were they out of sight, than Greybeard
quickly dropped to the ground, untied the bull, and
led him away to the hut.

" Here, friends," he called out to the old people,
" here is food in plenty. Kill the bull; we will have
a good roast of beef. You can then salt down the
rest, and make candles out of the fat; but his skin
you must keep for me!"

The delight of the old people, at the prospect of
such a supply of good food, can well be imagined.

The king's servants meanwhile, having gone back

to the first oak tree and finding no one there, had returned to the second tree, but when they found that both the bull and Greybeard had disappeared, they began to realize that a trick had been played upon them. So there was nothing to be done but to return to the palace and tell the king what had happened.

After hearing their tale, the king at once sent a messenger to Greybeard, telling him to come with all possible speed to the palace.

The old couple greatly feared, when they heard his message, that some evil was intended towards Greybeard, and quite expected the king would hang him.

But Greybeard told them to keep up a good heart and not to weep; and, whistling cheerfully, he appeared before the king without any sign of fear or dread.

"Was it you who stole my bull?" asked the king.

"I did not steal it, sire; I had to take it, in order to save my life," replied Greybeard.

"Well," said the king, "I suppose that is true, I will therefore pardon you again, if you can this night manage to take away the scepter from under my pillow without waking either the queen or me."

"That is beyond the power of any man to do," replied Greybeard; "for how can I get at night

into your palace, which is always guarded? much
less into your bedchamber!"

"Nay, that is your affair; you must see to that,"
replied the king. "And remember that, if you fail,
it means losing your life." And with these words
he dismissed him.

Then Greybeard returned to the old couple, who
welcomed him as if he had indeed returned to them
from the dead. Trude had roasted the finest joint,
gathered a big bowl of whortleberries, and baked
some nice crisp griddle-cakes, so they had a great
feast, after which Greybeard asked her to give him
one of her nice sleeping-potions which she made for
Geir when his rheumatism was very bad.

"That I will gladly, my son," said Trude, heartily.
She quickly hung her pot over the glowing embers,
putting in henbane and many other herbs, and when
the potion was ready she poured it into a little bottle
and gave it to Greybeard.

The sun had by this time set like a golden ball,
tinting the great brown stems of the tall pines with
a rich crimson glow, as Greybeard, with the bottle
carefully placed in his coat pocket, made his way
back to the castle.

Watching his opportunity when the sentry at the
little postern gate had turned his back, he slipped
through the gate and hid himself in a dark corner

behind one of the great buttresses. Presently he
heard the gates close for the night, so that there
should be no possibility of a thief getting in.

When Greybeard thought he had allowed a sufficiently long time to pass to admit of every one, in-
cluding the king and queen, being soundly asleep,
he stole quietly and cautiously out of his hiding-
place and along the great passages, till he reached
the royal bedchamber. Carefully opening the door,
he crept softly up to the big couch on which reposed
the king and queen. Making sure that they were
sound asleep, he drew forth his little bottle, poured
some of the contents on his handkerchief, and
dropped it lightly over the faces of the royal couple.

He waited for a few minutes to see that the sleep-
ing-drops had taken effect, and then, slipping his
hand under the king's pillow, he slowly and cautiously drew forth the great golden scepter, buttoned
it safely inside his coat, and, removing the handkerchief, he hastened back to his hiding-place behind the buttress, and as soon as the gate was
opened at daybreak, he ran back to old Geir's hut.

The next morning, when the king and queen
awoke, the former put his hand under the pillow,
and behold the scepter was gone!

"Ah, that rascal has been too clever for us
again!" cried the king, and immediately sent another

messenger to Greybeard to summon him to the castle at once.

This time Geir and Trude made sure the king would hang Greybeard, and were almost heart-broken as they bade him farewell.

"Did you yourself steal the scepter from under my pillow last night while we were asleep?" asked the king.

"Yes, oh king," replied Greybeard. "I did not steal it, however; but took it, as you told me. I had to do it to save my life."

"Well," said the king, "you certainly are a clever fellow. I will therefore pardon you all you have done if this night you can carry off both the queen and me, out of our bed. If, however, you fail to do so, you shall certainly be hanged without hope of forgiveness."

"That is not possible for any one to do unassisted," said Greybeard.

"Oh, that is your affair; see you to that," answered the king, and dismissed him.

Greybeard returned to his hut. The old people were greatly rejoiced to see him, for they quite expected the king would have hung him; but he was more silent than usual, and after they had finished their evening meal, and the old people had gone to bed, Greybeard went out and walked in the moonlight under the tall trees, planning how to carry out the fresh task given him.

Presently he returned to the hut and took down the old man's wide-brimmed felt hat that hung on a nail at the back of the door. Boring holes in the brim, he stuck in them some of the candles which Trude had made from the fat of the bull, and also fastened candles in his belt, and then, taking the great leather sack which Geir had made out of the bull's skin, he returned to the palace and stood in front of the chapel steps which faced the king's bed-room. Laying down the sack, he lighted all the candles he had brought, sticking them on his shoulders and wherever he could fasten them, and then rang the chapel bell.

This unusual sound in the middle of the night wakened the king and queen. Jumping hurriedly out of bed, they hastened to the window, and there, standing outside the chapel door, they saw a fig-ure, all blazing with light. Greatly startled, they thought it must be a spirit.

"Such a visitor must be received with all honor," said the queen. "Let us go out and ask his protec-tion and goodwill."

So they put on their very grandest clothes and went out to meet the supposed spirit. Falling on their knees, they begged him to tell them why he

had come, and hoped he would not be too severe
with them, or want them to give away too large a
portion of their treasure. Greybeard, looking very

stern beneath the light of the blazing candles, said
he did not want any of their money, but they must
both get inside the sack which he placed on the
steps.

" Is that all ? " cried the king, quite relieved.
" Why, that is very easily done ! " And, helping
the queen in first, he crept in after her.

But no sooner were they both inside than Greybeard pulled to the string. In vain the king kicked
and threatened, the queen adding her cries and
tears. Greybeard quietly blew out all the lights,
and dragging the sack rapidly across the yard,
said—

" I am no spirit, oh king, but your old friend
Greybeard. You see, I *have* got you and your queen
out of your beds as you commanded me to do, and
now it is for me to make my conditions. I will not
let you out of the sack unless you promise me your
forgiveness for what I have done, and also give me
your royal word that you will grant the request I
will presently make you."

The king was so frightened and helpless, fearing
that he might die ere Greybeard opened the sack,
that he willingly gave his royal word to grant his
request, whatever it might be. Whereupon Greybeard untied the sack, and when the king and queen
had crept forth, looking very crestfallen, Greybeard
said that, as next day was the princess's wedding-day,
he had now to demand the hand of the fair Sigrid
in marriage, as well as the half of the kingdom
during the king's lifetime ; and, further, that old

Geir and his wife who had befriended him in his poverty, should also live at the palace, and be amply provided for.

The king, having given his royal word, could not of course retract, so he and his queen returned to the palace very sad and sorrowful, for now, instead of having the rich old king for a son-in-law, they had to accept this terrible stranger and lose the half of their kingdom as well.

Greybeard meanwhile returned to the cottage, and when he told Geir and his wife that instead of losing his life he was going to marry the princess the next morning, and that they also were to be provided for, they could hardly believe his words.

" And now you must put on these smart clothes I have brought you, and go back with me," added Greybeard ; and as soon as the old couple were ready, they returned with him to the palace.

The morning of the wedding rose bright and sunny, and the old king, who had arrived, was lodged in the palace. Leaving Geir and Trude among the assembled guests, Greybeard went down into the beautiful gardens, and there, seated on the stone bench near the fountain, he saw Sigrid, looking sad and pale. She had heard of the gray stranger and all his wonderful doings, and though glad that she was not to marry this ugly old king, she could not forget Olaf.

Hearing a step approaching, she looked up and saw Greybeard coming towards her.

"Fair princess," he said, kneeling down before her. "Do not fear me, but lay your hand in mine and trust me; believe me, I only wish to make you happy."

His voice was so soft, and he spoke so gently, that Sigrid, despite his ugly gray beard, after a moment's hesitation, placed her hand in his. No sooner, however, had she done so, than the quaint gray figure disappeared. Behold! Olaf himself stood before her and with a glad cry she threw herself into his out-stretched arms.

Together they then hastened to the king and queen, and Olaf told them how, by the aid of his fairy godmother, he had been able to help the old couple who had fed and sheltered him, and also to claim his cousin's hand, when his year of travel was ended.

The king having given his word, there was nothing further to be said, and the old king had to return to his own country.

The wedding was one of the grandest that had ever been seen, and the feasting lasted a whole month. Olaf and Sigrid lived long and happily together, and

after the king's death Olaf succeeded to the kingdom, which he ruled with such wisdom and goodness, that his reign has ever since been known as
"The reign of King Olaf the Good."

LITILL, TRITILL, THE BIRD, AND THE PEASANT LAD.

THERE once reigned a king and a queen, and in the same country there also lived a poor old man and his wife. The king had an only daughter, called Enid, who was greatly beloved by both her father and mother. They spared no expense, and she had the best masters and governesses, and a number of servants to wait upon her; but notwithstanding that she was so carefully watched and looked after, she suddenly disappeared. The head governess said she had left her in her room only for a few minutes practising her harp, with two of her maidens in attendance, and when she came back she found both the girls fast asleep, and the princess gone. Inquiries were made of every one, but nothing could be heard of the princess. No one had seen her; she had vanished in the most mysterious manner. The king, in despair, sent out messengers in all directions, and spent a great part of his treasure searching for her; but all in vain. Then, at last, he vowed that he would give the princess in marriage to whoever should be fortunate enough to find her, and also give him the half of his kingdom. But though many of the knights and nobles about the court, eager to secure so great a prize, went off in search of her, they one and all returned empty-handed.

Now, the poor old man who lived outside the palace grounds had three sons. Their names were Osmond, Tostig, and Harald. The two eldest boys were greatly beloved by their parents; but Harald, the youngest and handsomest, was disliked by his father and mother, and both his elder brothers ill-treated him and made him do all the work, while they went out shooting and fishing.

When the boys were grown up, Osmond came to his parents, and said he would like to start off and see the world, and try to win fame and riches for himself.

His father and mother were quite willing he should do so, and providing him with a new pair of boots and a large bag of food, he started off on his journey.

After he had gone a long, long way, he arrived at a little hillock. Here he sat down to rest, and unpacked his bag of provisions.

Just as he was beginning to eat, a tiny little man, dressed in gray, came up to him, begging for a morsel of food. Osmond angrily ordered him away, threatening to beat him if he did not go quickly.

After he had rested, Osmond went on again a long, long way, till he came to another hillock. Here he again sat down to rest, and began to eat. But he had hardly commenced than a still smaller and shabbier little man, dressed in green, came up to him and asked him for a morsel of food. Osmond spoke angrily to him, and sent him away with a volley of abuse.

He then went on again a long, long way, till he reached a large open glade in the wood. Here he sat down on the soft, mossy grass at the foot of a big beech tree, and thought he would eat another morsel. But no sooner had he opened his bag and taken out the food, than a whole flock of birds flew down beside him; but he angrily chased them away, and then, having rested himself, went on his way, till he came to a big cave. Looking in, and seeing no one, only a lot of cattle, he thought he would go in and wait till the dawn arrived.

Just as the sun was setting, an enormously big giantess walked in. Osmond was greatly startled, but, taking courage, he went up to her, and asked whether he might stay the night there.

The giantess said yes, on condition that in the morning he would do the work she would require of him. This he promised he would do; so she allowed him to remain the night, she herself retiring into an inner cave.

The next morning the giantess told him that he must clean out the cave, and put down fresh bedding for the cattle, and that he must have it all finished before the evening, else she would take his life. With these words she went away.

Osmond took up a prong he saw standing in a corner, but no sooner did he begin to turn up the straw than the prong stuck fast in the bedding. In vain he pushed and pulled and tried to drag it out, the prong remained firmly fixed; and when in the evening the giantess came home and found that the cave had not been cleaned out, she took hold of Osmond and hung him up to a nail in the cave.

Meanwhile Tostig, the second son, thought he, too, would like to go out into the world to seek his fortune, for he felt sure his brother by this time must be quite a rich man. So he told his parents that he did not care to remain at home now his elder brother was away, and with only that stupid Harald at home; so having gained their consent, he, too, started off, provided with a pair of new boots and a big bag of provisions.

But he was not more fortunate than Osmond had been. He flouted the little men while he rested on

the hillocks, he chased and killed some of the birds
who came flocking round him for crumbs ; and when
he reached the cave, he also received leave from the
giantess to remain the night, on condition that he
cleaned out the cave next morning. When he went
and took up the prong to throw out the old bedding,
it stuck fast in the straw, and no efforts of his could
move it. So the giantess coming home, and finding
that he had failed to accomplish his task, took him
and hanged him beside his brother.

So now there was only the youngest son, Harald,
left. But though he was the only one at home, his
parents did not love him any better, and the poor lad
often felt that his presence reminded them of their
lost sons, and that they regretted not having sent
him away in their place. So he also decided to go
away.

"I do not suppose I shall win riches and fame.
All I hope is that I may be able to earn enough to
support myself, and be no longer a burden to you."

Then his parents told him he might go; but instead of nice strong new boots, they only gave him
an old pair of his brother's, and his sack contained
nothing but some hard, dry crusts.

But Harald started off with a light heart, and as
it chanced he, too, took the same road his brothers
had done, and presently he came to the first hillock.

"I think my brothers must have rested here, if they felt as tired as I do," he said, "so I will do the same." And seating himself on the hillock, he began to eat one of his dry crusts, when, looking up, he saw a little old man in gray standing beside him.

"HARALD PITIED THE OLD MAN."

"Will you share your crust with me? I am very hungry, and have had no food to-day," he said.

Harald pitied the old man, who looked so feeble and tired. He begged him to sit down beside him and share his meal. When they had done, the old man got up, and, after thanking him, said, "My name is Tritill. Although I am old and feeble, if

ever you are in need of help, call me, and I will
come to you." So saying, he went round the back
of the hillock and disappeared.

Harald then continued his journey till he came to
the second hillock.

"I feel sure my brothers must have rested here,"
he said. "It is a long way from the last hillock.
I, too, will rest here awhile." And he sat down, and
opening his bag, took out another crust. Hardly
had he done so when a tiny, shabby, little old man,
dressed in green, came up to him and asked for a
morsel of food. Harald very good-naturedly asked
him to sit down beside him, and shared his crust
with him. When they had finished eating, the little
green man got up, and, after thanking Harald, said—

"Call me, if ever you think I can do you a service.
My name is Litill." And he, too, went away, and
was soon out of sight.

Harald then continued his journey until he came
to the large open glade in the wood.

"I am sure my brothers must have rested here,"
he thought. "I will do the same." And he sat
down and took out another crust. No sooner had
he done so than a great flock of birds came down.
They circled round and round him, and seemed so
hungry and fought so eagerly over every crumb he
threw them, that Harald's heart was filled with

pity. "Poor little things!" he said; "they need it more than I do." And he broke up the remaining crusts and threw the crumbs among them.

When they had eaten up every crumb, the biggest bird alighted gently on Harald's shoulder and whistled softly—

"If ever you think we can do you a service, call us. We shall hear you wherever we are, for we are *your* birds." And ere he had recovered from his astonishment, they had all flown away and were out of sight.

Harald then continued his journey, until he, too, came to the big cave. Looking in, he saw it was full of cattle, and hanging from a beam in one corner he saw the bodies of his two brothers.

Startled at the sight, Harald's first impulse was to go away; but he thought he must first bury his brothers. So he took down the bodies, and seeing a spade near the entrance, he speedily dug a grave and buried them in the sand outside the cave. Just as he had finished, the giantess arrived.

Harald, who was very tired, asked her if he might stay the night there.

"You may do so, if you will promise to do what I tell you in the morning," answered the giantess.

This Harald agreed to, and he slept that night in the cave.

Next morning, the giantess, who had slept in an inner cave, told him that he would have to clean out the cave, and put down clean bedding for the oxen.

" But remember, if your work is not finished when I come home, I shall hang you the same as I did your brothers ; " and so saying she went away.

Harald took up the prong standing in the corner and began his work. But no sooner had he pushed the prong into the bedding and tried to lift it than it stuck fast to the ground. In vain he used all his strength, the prong remained firmly fixed. In his despair he called out : " Oh, dear Tritill, come and help me ! "

No sooner had the words passed his lips than he saw Tritill standing beside him, who asked what he could do for him. Harald showed him the difficulty he was in.

Then Tritill called out : " Prick prong and shovel spade ! " and immediately the prong pricked up the bedding and the spade shoveled it away, till in a very short time the cave was all cleaned out and fresh straw put down. Harald thanked him warmly for his help, and Tritill went away.

When the giantess came home in the evening and saw that the work was done, she said to Harald—

" Oh, man, man ! you have not done this by your-

self!   But I will let it pass!" and she retired into
the inner cave.

The next morning the giantess told Harald that
she had some fresh work for him to do.   He was to
carry her own bedding outside the cave, take out all
the feathers, spread them out in the sun to air, and
then put them back again.

"But remember, if when I come back in the evening there is a single feather missing, I shall hang
you as I did your brothers!" And with these words
she went away.

Harald carried out the great featherbed and the
big pillows; and as the sun was shining warm and
bright, and there was not a breath of wind, he
ripped open the seams and spread out the feathers
in the sun.

No sooner had he done so than a strong wind
arose, and in one moment all the feathers were
whirled away, not a single one remaining.

In despair Harald called out: "Dear Tritill, dear
Litill, and all my dear birds—oh, come and help me
if you can!" And almost before the words had
passed his lips, Tritill, Litill, and the whole flight of
birds, came bringing the feathers with them; and
while Tritill and Litill helped Harald to fill the bed
and the pillows, and sew them up again, the birds
flew round picking up all the stray feathers, so that

none were missing. But out of each pillow they took one feather, and, tying them together, told Harald that when the giantess missed them and threatened to kill him, he was to tickle her nose with the feathers.

Thereupon Tritill, Litill, and the birds all disappeared.

When the giantess came home in the evening, she went up to her bed, and threw herself down on it so heavily that the whole cave shook. Then she began carefully feeling all over the bed, and when she came to the pillows she cried out—

" Aha, man ! I have caught you—there is a feather missing in each pillow ! Now I shall hang you like your brothers ! "

But as she took hold of him, Harald quickly pulled the two feathers out of his pocket and tickled her nose with them.

In an instant the giantess fell back on her bed, looking terribly white and frightened ; but Harald laughingly gave her back her feathers, telling her he did not want to keep them.

" Ah, man, man ! " said the giantess, " I know you did not do this alone ; but I will let it pass this time ! "

So this third night Harald also passed in the eave, and in the morning the giantess said to him—

"I have some fresh work for you to-day. You must kill one of my oxen. Then you must scrape and clean the skin to make a leather bag ; cut up the animal in joints ready for cooking ; clean all the entrails, and make spoons out of its horns. All must be finished ere I return this evening. I have fifty oxen, as you see, and it is one of these I want killed. I shall not, however, tell you which one I have fixed upon ; that you must find out for yourself. If all is done as I wish when I return, you can depart in the morning and go wherever you like ; and in addition, as a reward, you may choose three things from among such of my treasures as I value most. If, however, everything is not finished, or if you kill the wrong animal, then it will cost you your life, and I shall hang you the same as I did your brothers." And so saying the giantess departed.

Harald was sorely puzzled. How could he possibly decide which of the animals the giantess wished killed ? Then he remembered his friends.

"Dear Tritill, dear Litill, come once again to my aid," he cried.

Hardly had the words passed his lips, than he saw them both coming towards him, leading a huge ox between them. They at once set to work and killed him, and while Harald cleaned the entrails and cut up the joints, Tritill scraped the skin and prepared it for making the bag, and Litill began fashioning the spoons out of the horns.

So the work sped along quickly and merrily, and all was ready ere the sun sank to rest.

Harald now told his friends what the giantess had promised him if he should have finished his task ere she returned.

"Can you advise me what to ask for?" he said.

Then they told him he should first ask for that which was over her bed, then for the chest which stood beside her bed, and lastly for that which was behind the wall of her bed.

Harald thanked them warmly for all they had done for him, and said he would do as they had told him, whereupon the little men disappeared.

When the giantess came home in the evening and found that Harald had finished all the tasks she had set him, she exclaimed—

"Ah, man, man! you never did all this alone; but you have conquered, so I must let it pass." And so saying she retired to rest.

The next morning, the giantess called Harald into the inner cave and told him he might choose the reward she had promised him, and that then he might go where he liked.

"Then," said Harald, "if I may have whatever I like, I choose, first, that which is above your bed; then the chest which is beside your bed; and, lastly that which is behind the wall of your bed."

"Ah, man, man!" cried the giantess. "You have not chosen these things by yourself; but I cannot refuse you; you are too strong for me, and you have conquered, and I must give you the reward you claim."

So saying, she mounted some steps above her bed cut into the rock, and, opening a secret door, she led forth a beautiful maiden. This was none other than the fair Princess Enid, who had disappeared so mysteriously some time ago.

"Take her back to her father, and he will reward you as you deserve," said the giantess as she placed the princess's hand in that of Harald.

She then opened the lid of the chest beside her bed. This was filled with gold, pearls, and precious stones; and then moving aside the bed, she touched a secret spring, and the wall sliding back, they saw the blue sea, and anchored close to the cave lay a beautiful ship, completely fitted out, her sails all set, and her pennant flying, and possessing the power of sailing wherever its owner wished, without aid of either captain or crew.

When the giantess had handed him over these

gifts, she told Harald that he would henceforth be one of the happiest and luckiest of men.

Harald then carried the chest containing the gold and precious stones on board ship, and then having arranged some soft cushions for the Princess Enid, in the stern of the vessel, they quickly departed, and reached her father's country.

The delight of the king and queen on recovering their long-lost daughter can be more easily imagined than described. They never tired hearing of the wonderful adventures through which Harald had gone, and the king ordered a great feast in honor of the rescuer of his child, which ended with the wedding of Enid and Harald.

The king then made Harald his prime minister; and so well and so wisely did he rule the country, that on the king's death he was chosen to succeed him, and he and Queen Enid lived long and happily together, seeing their children and grandchildren growing up around them.

LAUGHING INGIBJORG.

CHAPTER I.

LONG ago, when giants and ogres still walked about the earth, in a far distant country, there once lived a king and queen. They had two children, called Thorwald and Ingibjörg; but before the children were grown up, the good queen died.

The king, who was very fond of his wife, was quite inconsolable at her death. He lost interest in everything, shut himself up in his own rooms, only coming out to sit and weep beside her grave.

This went on for so long, that at last his ministers came to him, and told him that everything was going wrong in his kingdom, and that there was a rumor abroad, that a neighboring prince, hearing that the king no longer took any interest in his affairs, meant to cross the water and take possession of the king's

throne and lands. They therefore begged him to
rouse himself and look out for another wife, and
either go forth and seek her himself, or else send
his ambassadors to try and bring back a suitable
princess.

At first the king would not listen to a word they
said, but after a time he saw that his ministers were
right, so he agreed to fit out some ships and send an
embassy to several other countries in order to find
some fair princess worthy to share his throne.

Soon after the ambassadors had started and were
once fairly on the high seas, a great storm arose.
The sky grew black as night, the thunder roared and
the lightning flashed, and the wind blew so strongly,
driving the ships in all directions, that the sailors
quite lost their reckoning ; their rudders were broken,
and they drifted about at the mercy of the winds
and waves. At length, after many days, they sighted
land ; but when they came near, they saw it was
quite an unknown shore.

The chief men of the expedition now disembarked,
in order to make some inquiries, leaving the sailors
in charge of the ships.

For some time they could see no sign of any human
habitation, and thought they must have landed on
some uninhabited island, but at length they arrived
at a small farm, consisting of a few wretched huts,

15

Not hearing a sound, and seeing no one about, they at first concluded the place was deserted; but when they reached the last hovel, an old woman came forth, who, despite her great age, was both tall and stately, and at once asked them who they were and whence they had come.

"We have been driven here by the storm," replied the leader, and he then proceeded to tell her the object of their search.

"You certainly have been very unfortunate so far," answered the old woman, "and I fear there is but little chance of your finding what you seek here."

While they were talking the sun had set, and as the weather showed signs of again turning stormy, the ambassadors asked the old woman whether she could give them shelter.

At first she absolutely refused, saying her miserable hut was not fitted to receive people accustomed to live in royal castles; but, as the storm increased, they continued to urge her to let them stay, till at length she consented and bade them enter.

What was their surprise and astonishment to find the inside of this apparently miserable hut richly fitted up like some kingly apartment.

Handsome skins covered the floor, soft couches

ran round the walls, which were ornamented with
richly chased shields and arms, and a bright fire
burnt cheerily on the hearth.

As soon as the men were seated, the old woman
laid the great oaken table which stood in the center,
and served the strangers with such dainty dishes as
might well befit a royal table.

"And do you mean to say that you live here all
alone?" asked the chief ambassador, during the
meal.

"I might almost say that I do," replied the
woman, "for besides myself there is no one here but
my only child Guda."

"And, pray, may we not see the maiden?" asked
the ambassador; for they were all wondering what
the girl, living alone with her mother in these strange
surroundings, would be like.

Again the old woman demurred; but the more she
pretended to hesitate, the more the ambassadors
urged her, till at last she consented, and said she
would bring her daughter.

When at last she entered by her mother's side,
the ambassadors were almost startled by her marvelous beauty.   Tall and fair, like a stately lily, with
a perfect wealth of golden hair, falling in shining
masses to the ground, Guda appeared before them
like the goddess Freya. Surely, they thought, no-

where could they find a lovelier maiden to fill the vacant seat beside the king's throne.

So, without further hesitation, they at once solicited her hand in marriage, in the king's name.

The old woman pretended to think they were only joking, and laughed at the idea of the king seeking a wife in a peasant's cottage, adding that poor girls like her daughter had better remain at home, for such grandeur was not for them, and their ignorance of the ways of the world only brought them to shame instead of honor.

The king's ambassadors, however, would not be put off, and the more the old woman declared she could not part with her daughter, the more determined they were to take her away with them. At last, seeing the men would take no refusal, she consented to let the girl go, on condition that they would bring her back again, if, on seeing her, the king did not wish to marry her.

To this the ambassadors agreed, and then they all retired for the night.

Next morning the men prepared to return to the ships, and the old woman said her daughter would be ready to accompany them when she had got her things together. Then, to their surprise, they found she had so many packages that it needed all the ships' crews to carry them to the shore and put them on board.

The mother and daughter now went down to the beach together, talking earnestly, but in such low tones that no one could make out what they were saying; but one man heard the old woman say, " Remember, you must send me back the big stone ; I will manage the rest."

And then they reached the shore, where the old mother kissed her daughter, and, bidding her good-by, wished her all good luck and prosperity.

Then the anchors were weighed, the sails were hoisted, and the vessels put out to sea, reaching their destination without any mishaps.

When the king heard that his ambassadors had returned, he went down to the shore, accompanied by all the chief officers of his court, to bid the travelers welcome, and when he saw the young girl whom the ambassadors had chosen for his queen, he was greatly delighted, for she was more beautiful than any maiden he had ever seen, and seemed as sweet and good as she was lovely.

He conducted her back to the palace in great state. There a magnificent banquet had been prepared, and soon after the wedding was celebrated, amid the rejoicings of the whole island. The feast lasted three days, and every one who saw the fair

Queen Guda in her rich and costly robes, seated on the throne beside her husband, declared no more beautiful queen could possibly have been found, and though the king had loved his first wife, he soon became so completely wrapped up in Guda, that her word was law in everything.

Some months after the wedding, a war broke out in a neighboring kingdom, belonging to a cousin of the king, who had, therefore, to start off and help him, as his enemies were too strong for him to fight them alone.

The king, therefore, ordered out his war-galleys, and, as he expected to be away some time, he, at the queen's request, handed her his royal signet ring, begging her to rule the kingdom during his absence, and be a kind and loving mother to his two children, Thorwald and Ingibjörg.

This Guda promised she would do. So the king took a tender farewell of his wife and children, and getting on board his ship, followed by his men, a strong wind rapidly carried the vessels out of sight.

For some little time after the king had left, Queen Guda was very kind to the children. She had them to dine at her own table, gave them fruit and sweets and toys, and often took them for drives in her beautiful chariot, with the cream-colored horses.

Then one day she asked them to go down to the shore with her and play some games.

It was a beautiful morning; the sun shone warm and bright, the blue sea was smooth and glistening like a great sheet of glass, and as the tiny wavelets

"QUEEN GUDA ROLLED THE STONE INTO THE SEA."

receded, the golden sands were strewn with lovely pink and violet shells and glistening feathery weeds of every hue and shade.

"Oh, Thorwald!" cried Ingibjörg, running up to her brother and laughing merrily, her arms filled

with long trails of crimson and green seaweed.
"Look how beautiful they are! Let us play at being king and queen, and I will make two lovely
crowns."

"No; come here, children," said the queen. She
had walked some little distance along the shore,
and now stood beside a big square stone.   Then, as
Thorwald and Ingibjörg came near her, she muttered, "Open, oh stone !"   And at these words the
great square stone parted asunder, showing a large
cavity inside, and before the children knew what
had happened, Queen Guda had pushed them both
in; the stone closed with a snap, and, giving it a
strong shove, she rolled the stone into the sea.

She then returned to the castle weeping, telling
her attendants that the children had run away, that
she had called them to come back, but all in vain,
they would not obey; so she now sent out messengers in all directions, pretending terrible grief at
their supposed loss.

CHAPTER II.

HOW THORWALD AND INGIBJÖRG FOUND THEMSELVES AT THE WITCH'S ISLAND, AND WHAT THEY DID.

THE two children meanwhile, when they felt the stone closing, tried their utmost to force it open. But all their efforts proved fruitless ; the stone remained shut, and the children soon felt, by the rapid motion, that they were fairly out at sea, for, being a magic stone, it floated on the surface of the water instead of sinking to the bottom. The waves tossed it about for many hours, but at length the children felt the motion getting less and less, until at last the stone lay perfectly still.

"I think we must be near land now," said Thorwald. "There is no motion at all."

"If you think that, why should not you say the same words the queen did ? " replied Ingibjörg.

So Thorwald waited a little longer in order to make sure it was not merely a temporary lull, and then he called out loudly—

"Open, oh stone ! "

And immediately the great stone parted asunder, and Thorwald saw they were close to the shore.

The two children then slipped out, and paddled through the shallow water to the land. But though they wandered along the fine dry sand for some distance, they could see no sign of any habitation. They therefore determined to try and build a little hut for themselves.

Now, Thorwald, although but a young lad, had always gone out hunting with his father, who had given him a small gun and hunting-knife. These and his flute, on which he played wonderfully well, the boy never parted with, and he therefore had them with him when he and his sister had gone out with the queen in the morning.

Fashioning a rough wooden spade out of some driftwood for Ingibjörg, he used his knife to such purpose that a large hole was soon dug in the dry sand. This he then covered over with branches cut from the brushwood on the rocks, and leaving his sister to collect dry wood for a fire, he went in search of some birds for their supper. But although successful in shooting a couple, there was, alas! no fire to cook them, and poor Ingibjörg, who was getting very hungry, looked sadly at the food they could not eat.

" You pluck and prepare the birds," said Thorwald,

" and I will go further inland and see if I cannot get some fire."

So saying, he went up a narrow valley instead of, as heretofore, keeping along the shore, and after he had gone some little distance, he came to a small miserable-looking farm. He could see no one about, so he climbed up the steep slanting roof of the center hut and peeped down the hole which served as a chimney.

There he saw an old, very ugly, and dirty woman, busily engaged raking out the ashes from the hearth. But he noticed that half the cinders tumbled down among her feet, instead of into the ashpan she held in her left hand. So Thorwald made certain that the old woman must be blind.

He determined, therefore, to enter quietly into the house, and carry off a few live coals. First slipping down the roof, he crept slowly in at the low door, and then, watching his opportunity, he crawled along the wall till he reached the hearth. Then, seeing a small iron cup, he carefully pushed some glowing coals into it, and seeing no one else about, he made sure the old woman was alone, and while she was still busy raking, he crept out of the hut, and, much pleased with his success, hastened back to his sister.

Ingibjörg was delighted when she saw him arrive,

and the fire being all ready laid, a bright flame soon shot up ; the birds were roasted, and the two children made a hearty supper, Ingibjörg's merry laugh sounding again as gay as ever.

Thorwald, somewhat tired with his day's work, asked his sister to make up a good fire ere they went to sleep, so that it might last all night. But, alas ! when they woke next morning the fire was out, so he had to go again to the old woman's farm to fetch more coals.

This time he begged Ingibjörg earnestly not to let the fire out ; but, alack ! the little princess, though very willing and anxious to please her brother, had not been accustomed to attend to fires, so, though doing her best by making up a huge fire ere she went to sleep, it was out in the morning.

Ingibjörg even tried to wake up very early in order to put on fresh wood ; but, despite all her efforts, each morning the fire was out, and Thorwald had to go every day to fetch fresh fire.

CHAPTER III.

THEIR FURTHER ADVENTURES AND ESCAPE.

THUS the brother and sister lived for some time on the birds and game that Thorwald killed; and Ingibjörg having made a net out of the long tough shore grasses, they also managed to catch some fish and crabs, and their days passed pleasantly enough, while every morning Thorwald went up the valley and brought away some live coals, without the old woman ever finding it out.

Once, after he had taken away the coals, he heard her mutter—

" Ah! those devil's children! they are a long time in coming, but arrive here at last they must, for I made Guda promise to send them in the stone, and she dare not disobey me. Ah! only let me once get hold of them, and I will very soon put *them* out of the way."

Thorwald thought these words must surely refer to himself and his sister, who had arrived there in such a strange manner. He was, therefore, very careful whenever he came to the hut for the fire coals, to make as little noise as possible. He sometimes scarcely dared to breathe for fear the old woman might discover him.

Meanwhile Ingibjörg, who had been very good about staying alone in their little hut, at last became very curious about the old woman, and begged and entreated Thorwald to let her go with him some day. Thorwald, though willing to please his sister, was afraid to trust her, for he knew that the sight of the queer old woman would make her laugh; but he found it very difficult to deny her anything within his power to grant, and when, therefore, she continued to beg him to take her, he at last consented on condition that, no matter what she saw or heard, she must promise him she would not laugh, as, if she did, it might cost them their lives.

Ingibjörg promised she would keep quite still; so the next day the brother and sister started off together for the old farm.

When they got there they climbed up the sloping roof, and, with another warning to keep silent, Thorwald let his sister peep down through the chimney hole. But, alas! what Thorwald had dreaded actually took place.

The old woman, who stood near the hearth, was raking out the ashes so vigorously, that not only did she send them all over the floor instead of into the ashpan, but she made such a cloud of dust that

she was soon completely covered from head to foot
with a coating of gray ashes, and began to cough
violently.

When Ingibjörg saw this, she could not repress
her laughter, and a merry peal rang out in the clear
air.

No sooner did the old woman hear this than she
chuckled gleefully.

"Ha! ha! ha! So those devil's children have
come at last, have they? Ho! ho! ho! what a
joke! Now I shall have them! Ha! ha! ha!"

And with these words she rushed out of the house.
She was so quick, that she came up to the children
just as they were sliding down the roof, and they
might even then have got away, but that Ingibjörg,
at sight of the old woman, could not stop laughing;
she thought her still more comical-looking when she
began to run.

But the laugh now turned to grief, for the old
witch pulled some strong leather straps out of her
pocket, and fastening them round the brother and
sister, she drove them back into the house. There
she shut them up in a lean-to, and secured them
firmly with another strap to two strong wooden
posts.

The children at first were terribly frightened
when they found they could not get away, and

Ingibjörg blamed herself greatly for having, through her foolish laughter, brought about this terrible pass.

But the old woman evidently did not mean to starve them, for presently she placed a big bowl of bread and milk before each of them, saying—

"Now eat all you can, and don't waste anything."

In the evening she again brought them food in plenty; and this went on for some days.

But, though they were not harshly treated, except that they were never untied, the children grew very weary and tired ; the room was almost dark, the only light coming through the hole in the roof, which also served as a chimney. On the third day, the old woman took one of each of their hands, and mumbling and gently biting their fingers, she muttered—

"No, no! Not fat enough yet!"

Thorwald, therefore, determined to make every effort in order to free themselves ; but this was no easy matter. At length, after many attempts, he succeeded in biting through the strap that fastened his hands. He was thus able to get at his hunting-knife, which he fortunately always wore beneath his tunic, so the old woman had not seen it, else she would certainly have taken it away. Then, waiting till night closed in and the old witch was asleep, he cut through the rest of the straps that bound him and his sister.

"But the old woman will run after us and catch us if she sees us," whispered Ingibjörg.

"I have thought of that too," replied Thorwald; "we must, therefore, make sure she is asleep." And, creeping cautiously along the floor, he bent over the old hag, who lay snoring in one corner on a great heap of skins.

"She is sound," he then whispered, turning to Ingibjörg, having first carefully placed another thick skin over the old woman. "We must get away ere she wakens. Come, sister; don't delay!" And, taking Ingibjörg by the hand, he hurried her out of the house.

"Now you wait behind that great stone," said he, "while I cut and widen this ditch which runs across the road." Then Thorwald set energetically to work with his hunting-knife, and ere long had cut a deep wide ditch, throwing up the loose earth to form a bank, which rose up between them and the hut.

By this time the old ogress had wakened up, and, not hearing a sound, began feeling about for the children. When she had tapped all round and could not find them, she began to scream and swear with rage, and ran out, calling loudly after them.

16

As soon as Ingibjörg saw her rushing along, her hair streaming wildly behind her, she could not help laughing out aloud.

" Ha ! so you are there, you bad wicked children ! " cried the ogress. " But only wait, just let me catch you, and *I* will teach you to run away ! You shall be put into the oven at once, for you are quite fat enough now, and then I shall have a good meal ! " So saying she ran along the path to where she heard Ingibjörg's voice, but, unable to see the ditch, she fell in headlong and broke her neck.

Thorwald did not wait to learn what happened, but as soon as he saw the ogress run after them and fall into the ditch, he took hold of Ingibjörg's hand, and together they raced back to the shore, very thankful that they were now safe from the old witch's clutches.

CHAPTER IV.

THE KING'S RETURN, AND QUEEN GUDA'S RELEASE FROM THE WITCH'S THRALL.

SEVERAL weeks now passed. Each morning Thor-wald first gave a look across the sea in hopes of seeing a ship or boat, and would then start off in search of birds and game, while, strangely enough, after the old witch's death their fire never went out, and Ingibjörg, by carefully attending to it, was able to keep it burning both day and night.

Sometimes, when no food was needed, the children having laid in a sufficient supply of game and fish, Thorwald would take his flute and play, while his sister plaited mats and baskets out of the long rushes that grew near the shore.

Thus it happened that one day, while the two children sat on the shore, they saw several ships sailing slowly past the island.

Thorwald, who had just put down his flute, now took it up again, and began playing as loud as he could.

The ships came gradually nearer.

"Oh, Thorwald!" cried Ingibjörg, clapping her hands, "see, they are coming nearer! Oh, play louder, louder!" and she joined her voice to his flute.

And sure enough, ere long, the largest of the vessels cast anchor close to the shore, the other ships still keeping out to sea at some distance.

And then, to the children's great joy, they saw their father standing on the deck. A boat was lowered, the king and one of his followers were quickly rowed to shore, and in a few more moments Thorwald and Ingibjörg were clasped in their father's arms.

Great was his surprise to find them on this lonely island, for he had heard nothing of what had happened in his own country during his absence, and it was only by chance that he had sailed close to the island, none of his people caring to come near it, as it was supposed to be the home of evil spirits; and when they heard the sound of the flute they thought it must surely be the song of some mermaids, wiling the king's fleet to destruction by their soft, sweet melodies.

But the king for some reason felt he must find out what it was, so had ventured near the land, the rest of his fleet keeping out to sea.

The king then asked his children how it was they

were there, and when he heard what had happened during his absence, he grew very wroth.

He at once took the children on board his own ship, and commanded his people under pain of instant death not to breathe a word to any one of what had occurred.

The fleet was then ordered to set sail and return home with all possible speed.   Arrived near his own island, the king chose a quiet and retired part of the shore, and there he landed the children in charge of his own attendant, telling him to keep them hidden till he sent him word to appear with them at court.

The fleet then departed and cast anchor at the usual landing-place.   Here the queen, arrayed in her richest garments and attended by all her maidens, came down to welcome the king, expressing great joy at his return.

The king appeared well pleased to be at home again.

" But where are the children ? " he asked ; " and why have they not come to meet me, as they always do ? "

" Alas, alas ! " cried the queen, putting her handkerchief to her eyes as if to hide her tears, but really because she was afraid to look at the king. " Poor, poor children !   Pray do not speak of them !   Soon after you went away, they suddenly got very ill, and though I watched and nursed them myself, the poor little things both died!" and Guda began to sob and cry in reality, for she greatly feared what the king might do if he ever heard the truth.

And no one dared say a word; for during the king's absence Guda, urged on by fear of her mother if she did not get rid of her stepchildren, and also thinking that she could only govern by making herself feared, had ruled the kingdom with great severity, so no one dared say a word against her, believing that the king was still devoted to her.

The king, wishing to get at the truth of the strange tale, pretended great sorrow at the news of the children's death.

"And where are the poor little things buried?" he asked. "I should like to see their tomb."

The queen tried to persuade him not to go. She said she was sure it would only increase his sorrow, and entreated him to desist.

But the more she urged him not to go, the more determined he was to see their tomb.

So at length Guda yielded, and herself accompanied him to the wood at the back of the palace, where, in a pretty open glade, she had caused a handsome mausoleum to be erected.

He greatly admired the beautiful carving on the

stone, but he never shed a tear, which somewhat surprised the queen.   Soon after they both returned to the palace, where the queen had had a banquet prepared to welcome home the travelers.

All during the feast the king still remained very silent and preoccupied, and next morning he again event to the mausoleum, and then said he meant to have the children's coffins taken out.

When the queen heard this, she threw herself on her knees before the king, and begged and entreated him not to thus further increase his pain and grief. But the king remained firm.   The door of the great mausoleum was thrown back, and two small coffins, handsomely ornamented with gold and silver, were brought forth.   But, behold, when at the king's order these were opened, instead of containing the bodies of the two children, they were filled up with stones !

The queen gave a great cry when she saw her wickedness had come to light.   She fell down at the king's feet, and, sobbing and praying for mercy, she confessed what she had done, adding that her mother, the old witch, had forced her to do it.

But the king was so angry that he would not listen to her words, and ordered her to be shut up in the castle donjon till the Volkthing decided what her punishment should be.

Meanwhile Thorwald and Injibjörg arrived at the palace, the king having sent a messenger for them, and great was the rejoicing among the people when they learnt their young prince and princess, whom they thought dead, were alive and once again among them all.

The children then told their story before the assembled nobles and vikings, and when Ingibjörg related how Thorwald had killed the old ogress, who had only been fattening them up in order to eat them, there was a flash of lightning, and a loud crash of thunder resounded through the great hall. The door at the lower end opened, and, to the surprise of every one, the queen, draped in a long glistening white robe, walked up the hall, and falling down at the king's feet, she raised her clasped hands towards him.

"Pardon and forgiveness, oh king!" she cried. "The spell that has nearly cost me my life, is at length broken! That terrible old ogress was not my mother, but a wicked fairy who, because she thought my mother had not treated her as well as the other fairies at my christening, condemned me, as soon as my mother died, to serve her and obey all her behests as long as she lived. Now that your brave boy has killed her, I am freed from her wicked spells. And now, oh my king, punish me for the

harm I have so unwillingly done ; but, oh, let me
live to prove my gratitude to you and yours ! "

Great was the surprise of every one at the queen's
story, and the ambassadors then recalled to mind
how silent and grave the young queen had been
when they first saw her, even while she did all the
old witch ordered her to do.

Thorwald also added his entreaties to those of the
queen, and when Ingibjörg with a merry laugh
threw one arm round her father and the other round
the queen, the king relented. And thereupon the
interrupted feast was renewed amid general rejoicing,
the queen seated at the king's right hand with
Thorwald beside her, and Ingibjörg on his left hand.

There was no happier family in all the land.
Queen Guda, having no children of her own, lavished
all her affection on Thorwald and Ingibjörg, whose
entreaties had restored her to her husband, and the
reign of the king and Queen Guda was ever after
cited as one of the longest and happiest ever known.

THE THREE PEASANT MAIDENS.

CHAPTER I.

HOW QUEEN HERTHA FELL FROM HER HIGH ESTATE.

IN a distant island, long, long ago, there lived a wealthy peasant, who had three daughters called Alitea, Truda, and Hertha. Alitea and Truda were both fine handsome girls, but Hertha, the youngest, was by far the loveliest of the three.

Their house was not far from the king's palace, and one day, when the three sisters were out walking, they met the king, attended by his secretary and his valet.

"Ah," sighed Alitea, the eldest sister, "how happy I should be if I could only marry the king's valet! I should then be able to see all the grand feasts that are held at the palace!"

"And I should like to marry his secretary," murmured Truda, the second sister, "for then I should both hear and see all that was going on."

250

" Oh, if I had to marry any one," cried Hertha, the youngest sister, " I should like to marry King Leofric himself! See how young and handsome he is ! "

The king, who had noticed the whispers and eager glances of the girls, said to his attendants—

" I wonder what those pretty maidens want ? Let us go to them and find out what they are talking about; I thought I heard them mention my name."

The secretary tried to dissuade the young king from speaking to the girls, saying he was sure their chatter was not worth listening to, and that his Majesty had better not attend to them. But King Leofric would not be put off, and it ended in their all three going up to the young maidens. Then the king asked them what they had been talking about when he and his attendants came in sight.

Now when the girls saw the king come up to them, they were rather frightened, but he spoke so kindly and pleasantly that their fears soon vanished, and when he insisted on hearing what they had said, they at last confessed the truth.

King Leofric was mightily amused when he heard their tale. He thought the girls very handsome, especially the youngest one, and after chatting with them for some little time, he found them so bright and clever, that he told them their wishes should be fulfilled.

The sisters were so surprised to think their idle
words should speedily become real facts, that they
were speechless with wonder and delight.

So the king and his two attendants escorted the
girls back to their home, where the father's pride
may be imagined when he heard who the suitors
were.   Of course he threw no difficulties in the way,
and as the king's wishes were law, all three maidens
were shortly married, each to the man of her choice.

Now, although Alitea and Truda would have been
quite satisfied with their choice had Hertha not become queen, no sooner did they realize how much
grander was her lot than theirs, than they became
very jealous of her, and though she did her best to
be friends with them, giving them handsome presents, and taking them everywhere with her, their
envy only grew stronger, till at last they determined
that, no matter at what cost, she must be brought
down from her high estate. So they plotted and
planned for many a long hour, how they could best
get her out of the way.

At the end of a year the queen had a little son.
Then her sisters took away the baby in the night,
and arranged that it should be cast into the deep
ditch outside the city walls, where all the rubbish
was thrown. But the old woman who had under-
taken to do this, thought she would give the poor

babe a chance for its life; so, instead of throwing it in the ditch, she placed it on the bank, hoping that some kind person passing might see it and take it away.

And this actually did happen, for Osric, a poor old woodcutter, on his way home, seeing the pretty babe lying there, crying helplessly, took it up in his arms.

"This is a strange thing," he said. "Some one surely must have put it here purposely. But I cannot leave the poor bairn crying here."

So saying, he carefully wrapped it in his old coat and took it home, where he fed it as best he could.

When next morning it was found that the baby had disappeared, the sisters told the king they were sure that the queen must have put away or killed the child; but, though King Leofric was greatly grieved at the loss of his little son, he loved his wife too dearly to blame her for the child's disappearance.

The next year the queen again had a baby boy, and the news caused great rejoicings all through the kingdom. But that same night this child also disappeared, and the two sisters again told the king that they were sure the queen had caused it to be killed.

But King Leofric, though startled and grieved

at these strange disappearances of his children, still trusted his wife and would not hear a word against her.

The following year, greatly to the king's delight, the queen had a baby girl.

"Surely," she thought, "this time nothing shall come between me and my baby." So she would not let the little creature out of her arms, day or night.

But she was weak and ill, and the second night, seeing she would not lay down the child, the wicked sisters gave her a sleeping-draught, and as soon as her eyelids closed, they again took away the babe and gave it to the old woman to throw into the ditch.

When next morning the king heard that his little daughter, at whose birth he had so rejoiced, had also disappeared, his grief and anger knew no bounds. They quite overcame his former love for his wife. He would listen to no excuses, and ordered her to be thrown into the den of the big lion.

When the wicked sisters heard this, they thought they had now got rid of Queen Hertha. They were quite pleased to think they had at last succeeded in the wicked plot they had planned, without the king or any one else ever suspecting the part they had taken in it.

CHAPTER II.

WHAT HAD BEFALLEN THE TWO LITTLE PRINCES AND THEIR SISTER.

But Queen Hertha was not dead ; for the lion, so far from hurting her, laid himself quietly down at her feet, and when his food was brought to him, he would never touch it till the queen had taken her share.

So, while every one thought she was dead, Queen Hertha lived beside her powerful friend. At first she had been terribly frightened, but she speedily grew almost to love the huge beast, who, when the king and her sisters had been so cruel, had befriended her in her hour of need. Still it was at best but a dreary existence, and many times and often she wished she could but know what was happening outside the lion's den.

As for the children, the same old man Osric, who had picked up the first baby, had fortunately also found the other boy and the baby girl, and had taken them home to his own little cot, near the woods, where he brought them up as well as he could. He called the elder boy Wilhelm, the second one Sigurd, and the little baby girl Olga.

He had tried at first to find out whose children they could possibly be, but one night he dreamed that a beautiful fairy came to his bedside, and said—

"Osric, if you love the children, don't ask any questions about them, but bring them up as your own—their enemies will else destroy them. Let them wait till they are grown up."

So he had kept his own counsel, and did the best he could for them. Strangely enough, too, he found that his barrel of meal never ran short, and with his cow and his little patch of garden ground they always had a sufficiency of food.

So the children grew up strong and healthy, the boys helping the old man in his forest work, and fetching the wood and water that was wanted; and as for Olga, she soon became quite an expert little housekeeper. But, though they wore rough, homespun garments, they were good to look at, for they all three inherited the marvelous beauty of their father and mother.

At last, when the young people were grown up, the old man, feeling his end draw near, called Olga and her brothers to his bedside. He then told them how and where he had found them, and also mentioned the strange vision he had had.

"But now that you are grown up," he added "I should advise you to make all inquiries, and not to rest till you have found out who and what you are, for I feel sure you are no ordinary children." Thereupon he gave them his blessing and died."

Wilhelm, Sigurd, and Olga sorrowed deeply over the death of their kind foster-father, for they had loved him dearly. When they had buried him in the forest, they returned sadly to the empty hut and consulted together as to what they had best do in order to carry out his instructions.

While they were thus sitting and talking, the door of the hut opened, and an old man entered. He was dressed entirely in green ; his hair was long and white, so also was his beard, and in his hand he carried a thick oaken staff.

" Good-morrow, father," said Willhem ; " you are welcome, though we have not much to offer you. Pray take a seat and rest, for you look weary."

" I have come a long way, my son," answered the old man ; " but though I am still hale and hearty, I shall not be sorry for a short rest. But you seem in sorrow or trouble," he added, looking from one to the other. " Perhaps I might be able to help you, for I have traveled far, and seen many strange and wonderful things."

17

"We shall indeed be glad of some advice," said Sigurd, while Olga hastened to place a bowl of new milk and some oatcakes before the traveler. "Sir we are sadly perplexed as to what we ought to do." And the brothers then proceeded to tell the stranger their story, and the advice their foster-father had given them.

When he had heard their strange tale, the old man said—

"I fear I cannot help you myself, but I think I know some one who may be able to advise you. You must know that about three days' journey from here, there lies a valley full of strangely shaped stones. In the middle of this valley there is a rock, on which a large bird sits, who is very wise, and understands and speaks the human language. Now, I think you should go and see this bird, though I will not conceal from you that there is very great danger attending such a visit. Many people have gone to consult him, but so far no one has ever returned. He is, however, so wise that he can both foretell the future, and also reveal the past. Many princes and others have gone for advice to this wonderful bird, but one and all have failed in carrying out the conditions, which can alone insure success. You must know that whoever mounts the rock on which the bird sits, must be so brave, and have such strength of will, that, no matter what he may see or hear, he must not turn round or look back; for if he does, even for only a second, he will at once be turned into stone. So far, no one yet has possessed the required purpose and unswerving staunchness," continued the old man; " but it is not difficult to mount the rock, provided you have the necessary determination. Then, when you *have* mounted, you will have the power to restore to life all those who, through lack of will and strength of purpose, were turned into stone, for on the summit of the rock there is a huge jar filled with magic water, and he who safely reaches the summit may take some of this water, and sprinkle it over those who have been turned to stone; they will then awake to life, and regain their form and figure."

Both brothers thought the task by no means a difficult one, and declared themselves quite ready and willing to undertake the journey. They thanked the old man heartily for all his information and advice and then sped him on his journey.

Next morning Wilhelm said to Sigurd that he would start forth in search of the rock. But before he left, he said to his brother—

" If at any time you see three drops of blood on your knife when you are at dinner, you must get up and follow me, for you will then know that I have failed, and have been turned to stone, and that you must then try your best."

So Wilhelm went forth, followed by the good wishes of Sigurd and Olga. But after three days, when the brother and sister sat down to dinner behold three drops of blood were on the blade of Sigurd's knife!

Hastily starting up, he told Olga he must be off at once in search of their brother.

"And remember, Olga, though I hope I may be successful, if at the end of three days you see three drops of blood on your knife, you will know that I too have failed."

He then bade her a loving farewell; and Olga saw him start on his way, with many fears and prayers in her heart for his safety.

CHAPTER III.

OLGA'S COURAGE RESCUES HER BROTHERS, QUEEN HERTHA
IS RESTORED TO HER HUSBAND, AND THEIR PARENTS
RECOVER THEIR CHILDREN.

IT seemed to Olga as if the time would never pass.
Each day seemed longer than the last, and when
the morning of the third day arrived, she had scarcely
courage to look at her knife as she sat down to her
breakfast.

But, oh joy! the blade was bright and clear, and
with a light and happy heart, she went about her
daily tasks.

When midday approached, she again glanced anxiously at the table, but, to her intense relief, the
knife beside her plate was undimmed by either spot
or stain, and feeling as if a great weight had been
lifted off her, she sat down to her spinning-wheel,
which she had not had the heart to do before, and
hummed one of her favorite ballads, to drive away
the feeling of loneliness that crept over her.   And
thus the hours passed; then, as the long, slanting
rays of the sun warned her that the day was nearly
over, Olga put away her spinning-wheel, and got

ready her supper.   She had placed her plate of por-
ridge on the table, and, bringing a bowl of milk
from the cupboard, had just seated herself, when,
glancing down, she saw three bright crimson drops on
the knife beside her plate !

With a cry of grief and horror, Olga sprang up.
There was now no thought of food or rest.   Not a
second must be lost if she hoped to save her
brothers !

Hastily putting on her cloak and hood, she hurried
out into the forest, following the path she had seen
her brothers take.

Evening was closing in, and the tall trees cast
dark and weird shadows around her.   But never for
a moment did Olga hesitate or rest.   Strange uncouth
sounds seemed to fill the air, and she could almost
fancy that the clinging brushwood which often
crossed her path seemed like long arms trying to
hold her back.   But she had only one thought,
one resolve—the rescue of her brothers ; so she
kept bravely on, putting aside every obstacle that
obstructed her way.

At length, after a long and weary journey, Olga
arrived at the valley in which stood the great
rock.   As she came near, she saw that the whole
ground was covered with innumerable stones of
quaint and varied forms.   Some looked like people,

some like animals, and one tall figure had several square stones at his feet, like chests or boxes.

But Olga, though her heart almost jumped into her mouth at the wild, weird scene, walked courageously forward, turning neither to the right nor left till she reached the rock on which sat the bird, his crest raised fiercely, while angry flashes of light from his eyes almost blinded her. No sooner, however, had her foot touched it, then a loud rumbling noise arose, wild cries and screams filled the air, thunder pealed, and flash after flash of lightning filled the valley with a lurid light, strong arms caught hold of her and tried to keep her back, while entreaties for help sounded on every side. Once, indeed, she distinctly heard her brothers' voices, praying her to look round if she loved them. Steadfastly, however, with a prayer on her lips for strength and guidance, Olga went bravely up the rock.

No sooner had she reached the summit, than immediately the thunder and lightning ceased, the weird cries and screams were silent, and, as she approached the great bird, he lowered his angry crest, and in a soft voice, praised her for her courage and steadfastness.

" I can now tell you whatever you desire, and will gladly help you in any way you wish," he added.

Then Olga asked that she might first of all be
allowed to restore to life all those who had been
turned to stone.

This the bird readily granted, and, filling the lid
of the stone jar with some of the life-restoring water,

"OLGA WENT BRAVELY UP THE ROCK."

Olga lost no time in sprinkling all the strangely
shaped stones with the magic water.

They all immediately regained their natural forms;
the still and silent valley soon reechoed with the
sound of voices, and as the girl stood there between

her two rescued brothers, all the others came up to thank the fair and brave maiden whose courage and steadfastness had rescued them from their stony prison and restored them to life.

" And now," said Olga, turning again to the wonderful bird, " can you tell us whose children we are ? "

" You are the children of the king of this country," he replied ; and then proceeded to tell them how the two wicked aunts, through jealousy, had caused them to be carried away, and had then accused their mother of destroying them, for which supposed misdeed she had been thrown into the lion's den.

" But," he added, seeing the grief and horror of the young people, " the lion's mouth was closed, so that, instead of killing her, he not only shares his food with her, but has so guarded the cage that no one dares enter ; she is still alive, therefore, though almost at death's door through grief and all the anxiety she has endured."

Then one of the strange figures who had been restored to life, and whom Olga had especially noticed as being taller and fairer than most of the others, and also because he was surrounded with several quaintly shaped chests, now came forward. He was a handsome young fellow, and stated that he was called Odo, and was the son of a neighboring king, and that, having gone forth in search of treasure and adventures, he had succeeded in amassing a large quantity of gold and precious stones, and was on his way home, when he heard of the wonderful bird, who could foretell the future. He had gained the valley and was almost close to the bird, when he incautiously looked back, hearing wild cries for help, and in that moment he had been turned to stone, and his were the quaintly shaped chests Olga had noticed.

The bird, being in a gracious mood, allowed the prince to carry away his treasure; so, followed by his servants, he accompanied Olga and her brothers to their home.

As soon as they arrived, they at once went to the lion's den and liberated the poor queen—the lion offering no resistance—and took her back to their hut. Poor Hertha was almost dead with grief and anxiety; but loving care quickly restored her to health, and the delight of seeing her dear children, whom she had thought dead, alive and well before her, did more than anything to restore her and make her strong and well.

They then procured her some rich and fitting garments, and leaving her in the hut, they repaired to the king's court and demanded an audience.

After some little delay, this was granted, for after

the loss of his wife and children the king had grown sad and listless, often blaming himself for condemning his queen so hurriedly; for, when he had time to think it all over, he could not, despite her sisters' repeated representations, believe that the queen had really killed her children.

When the sister and brothers were ushered into the royal presence, the king was at once struck by their noble appearance, especially with Olga, whose likeness to her mother was marvelous.

They then told him who they were and how they had been saved, and also that they had just freed their mother, who was not dead, as he had been told.

King Leofric could scarcely believe he heard aright as they related their wonderful tale, the particulars of which they had received from the magic bird, and it is impossible to describe his delight and thankfulness to find that his wife, whom he had loved so dearly, was not only proved innocent, but was alive and well.

He immediately sent for her two wicked sisters, and when questioned as to what they had done, they began first to prevaricate, and then each accused the other of having done the wicked deed. But the truth was clearly proved against them, they were therefore both thrown into the lion's den, where the poor queen had so long lingered; this time, however, the lion never hesitated, but eat them both up at once.

The king then eagerly went to fetch his queen, who returned to the palace with all due honors and splendor.

A great feast was immediately prepared to celebrate the happy restoration of the lost queen and her three children.

This feast lasted many days, for all who chose to come were welcome; indeed, it seemed as if the king could not do enough to show how thankful he was.

He remitted the sentences of many state prisoners, and all the poor in the kingdom received rich gifts.

When at length the feast came to an end, Prince Odo asked the king for the hand of his daughter, the fair princess Olga.

Thereupon a fresh feast was arranged to celebrate the marriage of the prince and princess, and this was carried out with still greater splendor, such as had never been seen before.

Not only was the big hall of the palace prepared for the invited guests, but endless tables were spread in the great courtyard for all the poor and homeless, to whom abundant good fare was generously dispensed, for, Princess Olga said, as they had been poor themselves they must never forget their less fortunate subjects.

Then, when it was over, Prince Odo returned to his own kingdom with his wife, where they reigned in peace and happiness for many years.

Wilhelm married a beautiful cousin, and succeeded to the throne at his father's death. Sigurd also married a lovely princess in a neighboring state, and came to the throne on the death of his father-in-law.

Thus Olga and her brothers, after all their trials, lived long and happily, their children and children's children reigning after them for many generations.

THE FAIR AND THE DARK ISOLDE.

CHAPTER I.

THERE once reigned a king and queen, and they had one little daughter called Isolde. She was the loveliest little maiden ever seen; her skin was white as the driven snow, her cheeks looked as if pink rose-petals had fallen on them, her lips were the color of the reddest cherries, and the deepest blue of the summer sky seemed reflected in her eyes, while her long fair hair, reaching almost down to the ground, glistened like gold when touched by the sun's rays.

Having no son of his own, the king had adopted his nephew Fertram as his heir to the crown.

The boy was as handsome as the little girl was lovely, and his father and mother being both dead, he was brought up at his uncle's court.

He was two years older than Isolde; but the
270

children were devoted to each other, and the parents often looked forward to the time when they would be old enough to be betrothed and married.

But the truth of the old saying, " the best-laid plans of mice and men gang aft agley," was once again to be verified, for when Isolde and Fertram were respectively sixteen and eighteen, and there was talk of a great betrothal feast shortly, the good queen, who had gone out bathing in the sea on a raw autumn morning, took a severe chill and shortly after died.

The king was quite inconsolable at her loss, and after her funeral, he shut himself up in his rooms for many months and would see no one but Fertram and Isolde. Even when at length he again came forth, he seemed to take no interest in anything.

Gradually matters grew worse and worse, till at last the chief officers of the court came to him and advised him to marry again.

For a long time the king would not listen to them ; but at length, wearied out with their importunities, he said they might go and see if they could find any one worthy to succeed his late queen.

So some ships were fitted out, and the chief officers started forth on their quest, they sailed on for many days without seeing any land, but at length they saw some rising ground on the horizon, which, as they came nearer, proved to be a rocky island surrounded by a low sandy beach.

Here the men landed, and following a narrow road which led them up a thickly wooded valley, they presently arrived at the gates of a fine castle.

They looked to see if the warden was there, for the drawbridge was down; but no one was on the walls, so they crossed the bridge and blew the horn which hung near the gateway. Immediately the great doors flew open, and they entered.

Still there was no one about; so they walked up a wide flight of stairs, and presently they came out on a broad terrace. Here a handsome, tall, and stately woman, dressed all in black, came forward and bade them welcome; she then clapped her hands, and a pretty dark-haired maiden appeared, bearing a silver tray with flagons of rich wine and fruit.

The ministers were invited to sit down on one of the big stone benches, and while they were partaking of the fruit and wine, which was very welcome after their long walk, the lady told them that her husband had died in battle, most of his followers having also been killed, and that she was now living there alone with her daughter.

Then she brought out her lute, and sang to the men while they rested, and entertained them so well, that they all agreed they need go no further to seek a lady worthy to fill the late queen's place ; so they forthwith solicited her hand for their master the king.

At first the queen said she could not think of accepting the offer, for that she had made up her mind, after her dear husband's death, to live and die in his now deserted castle ; but the more reluctant she appeared, the king's ambassadors only grew the more urgent, until at length she consented to go with them.

Handing over the castle and all it contained to an old servant, she and her daughter departed with the king's people, and, the wind being favorable, the homeward journey did not take many days to accomplish.

When the king saw the ships in the distance all decorated with flags and gaily colored banners, he knew that the ministers must have been successful in their quest ; so he ordered out his golden chariot, and, accompanied by all his chief courtiers, drove down to the shore, there to await the travelers.

At length the vessels were beached, and no sooner had the king set eyes on his bride, than he at once felt a great love for her in his heart. He placed her beside him in his golden chariot, while her daughter and the attendants followed in a silver one.

18

And thus they proceeded back to the palace, where a great feast had been prepared, at which all the great princes and nobles of the land were present.

The rejoicings continued for a whole week; wine and mead were lavishly dispensed to all who came, and the tables literally groaned beneath the great dishes of fish, flesh, and fowl, interpersed with huge pyramids of delicate cakes and delicious fruits.

At the end of the feast, each guest was presented with valuable gifts from the king's treasure-house, so that all those who were poor when they came, returned home rich and happy, while the queen herself was invested with all the grandeur and power of her new position.

Strangely enough the new queen's daughter was called Isolde, like the king's daughter; but, though the former was very pretty, every one declared she could not compare with the latter. So, in order to distinguish them, the former was always spoken of as "dark Isolde" and the latter "fair Isolde."

Now Isolde, the king's daughter, did not live in the palace, for her father, on her sixteenth birthday, had built her a separate tower standing in the midst of a beautiful garden. It was fitted up with every possible luxury and convenience; rich curtains draped all the windows, soft couches, covered with dainty silks and cushions of cloth of gold, lined the walls, and bright carpets were spread on the inlaid, polished floors.

Here Isolde spent her days very pleasantly with her two favorite attendants Eya and Meya, spinning and weaving and gathering flowers to deck her rooms ; and here Fertram would often join her, after one of their long rides in the forest, chatting and laughing and making happy plans for their future.

Soon after the king's second wedding, the queen came to him one day, and, after praising his kind rule over his people, told him she thought he ought not to remain longer at home with her, but make a tour and visit all his provinces to see what the governors were doing, and whether they were getting in the treasure rightly.

The king, who was very happy and comfortable at home, did not at first agree to this ; but the queen at last managed to persuade him, and also advised him to take Fertram with him, saying that it was only right he should see something of the world, and of the kingdom over which he was one day to rule.

So at length the king yielded, and ordered his ships to be got ready, at the same time telling Fertram that he was to accompany him.

Though pleased at the thought of the journey, Fertram was grieved to leave fair Isolde, and the

parting between them was a very sad one, for both
felt that some misfortune was hanging over them,
and yet they could not tell what.

A few days later the king and Fertram sailed
away amid great cheering of the people, who crowded
down to the shore to wish the travelers good speed
on their journey and a quick and happy return.

CHAPTER II.

WHAT BEFALLS "FAIR ISOLDE" AFTER HER FATHER HAS GONE.

ISOLDE the fair felt terribly sad and lonely after her father's and Fertram's departure; she lost all interest in her work and play, and would sit for hours at one of the windows facing the sea, ever hoping to see the welcome sight of the returning ships.

At last, one morning about a fortnight after the king had gone, the queen came to her, and, greeting her kindly, asked her to come with her and her daughter, dark Isolde, and spend the day in the woods.

" I know a lovely spot," she added, " where we can have a splendid game of ball, and then, when we are tired, we can sit down and rest and dine beneath the shade of the trees."

Fair Isolde at first refused, saying she did not feel as if she cared to play ; but the queen would take no denial, and at last Isolde, who had been very lonely since Fertram went away, agreed to go, together with her two maidens Eya and Meya.

It was a fine bright morning as the whole party set forth, and the sun and the fresh air soon made Isolde feel more like her former self.

Laughing and singing, the whole party wandered merrily through the woods till they reached a lovely open glade, when they commenced a merry game.

Here, there, and everywhere flew the bright-colored balls, tossed and caught by eager hands.

Isolde the fair was more deft in her play than the others, and never missed a ball; but further and even further flew the balls sent by the queen and her daughter, till at length they and fair Isolde were quite out of sight of their attendants, when the latter, running swiftly after a bright crimson ball, suddenly paused, for at her feet there yawned a deep dark pit.

"Oh, stop!" she cried, startled, looking round at the queen and dark Isolde. "Stop! Don't come any further, or you will fall into this dreadful place!" But the words had scarcely passed her lips when she felt a strong push and fell headlong into the hole.

Then the queen, laughing wickedly, looked down at poor Isolde and said—

"Ha! ha! my pretty bird! How do you like your new house, fair Isolde? It is not quite so fine as your grand, beautiful tower, is it? But you won't

"'DON'T LEAVE ME HERE!' CRIED FAIR ISOLDE."
Page 279.

Icelandic Fairy Tales.

need such pretty things now, for you will soon be dead, and then Fertram on his return will marry my dark Isolde ! "

" Oh, help me out !   Don't leave me here ! " cried fair Isolde ; " and I will promise, on the word of a princess, never to speak of this to any one ! "

" No, no, my young damsel !   Promises are easily broken ; but the dead tell no tales ! "   And, despite her tears and entreaties, the wicked queen and her daughter placed branches of pine trees across the open pit, and then covered them thickly with earth and leaves, so that no one, even if they passed that way, would ever dream there was a grave hidden beneath.

By this time the sun had set, and it was getting dusk ere they had finished their task ; so the queen and dark Isolde hastened back to the palace, but ere they entered it, they set fire to fair Isolde's tower, which was soon completely burnt to the ground.

The queen's attendants, meanwhile, together with Eya and Meya, finding the queen and the two princesses did not return, called out and searched for them in various directions, but, seeing nothing of them, concluded they had returned to the palace, and so, as it was now quite dark, hastened home themselves.

On their arrival there, they found the queen and

dark Isolde, who said fair Isolde had returned with them back to her tower, saying she was tired, when shortly after, to their horror, they had noticed flames bursting out of the windows, but ere they could send help, the tower was burnt down.

Poor Eya and Meya were inconsolable at the loss of their beloved mistress, and mourned long and sadly for her.

CHAPTER III.

WE must now return to fair Isolde.

When she heard the queen's words and knew that they did not mean to help her, but intended leaving her there to die, she wept long and bitterly ; then, as hour after hour passed, and, though she listened intently, she could hear no one passing by who might have helped her, she sat down on a heap of leaves lying in one corner, and began to think how best she could get out. Then she suddenly remembered that she had fortunately that morning put on the golden girdle which had been a parting gift of her mother on her death-bed, and to which was attached a large pair of golden scissors. She had enjoined fair Isolde never to go outside the house without this girdle, for it had been given her by a fairy god-mother, and had the marvelous power of preserving whoever wore it both from hunger and fatigue.

Isolde, therefore, after her first burst of grief, felt she was not quite helpless; the power of the girdle would save her from starvation, till she could once again procure food. And meanwhile, feeling somewhat comforted, she took hold of the big golden scissors, and by working hard, and persevering in spite of fatigue, she managed to dig some deep holes in the side of the pit, large enough to give her a good foothold, and thus managed to climb up to the top, and work her way through the mass of earth and leaves the wicked queen and her daughter had piled up together.

When she at last got out, she wandered about the forest for some time, till she got back to the open glade, where they had played ball.

Here she sat down to consider what she had better do.

At first she thought it would be safer to keep hidden away in the forest, for fear her stepmother might find her and again try to kill her ; but, on second thoughts, she decided it would be better for her to return to the tower, and so disguise herself that no one could possibly recognize her.

She first stained her face brown with the juice of some berries, and then with her deft fingers she made herself a quaint dress and large cap out of various colored leaves, and thus disguised, she went back to her tower, and found it a heap of ashes. Feeling now certain there was a plot against her, she determined to go on to the palace, went round to the kitchen door, and begged the cook to give her a morsel of food, as she was very hungry.

The cook, who was a kind-hearted old woman, told her to sit down on a bench, and fetched her some bread and meat, in return for which, Isolde offered to mend her clothes for her, as she probably had no time to do so herself, saying her name was Näfra Kolla, the sewing girl.

The old cook, who, although good at her own work, was no great hand with her needle, was delighted when she heard this, and told her she was welcome to stay as long as she liked, more especially as the king would soon be back, when there would be plenty of work for every one.

So Näfra Kolla remained, and when it was seen how clever she was with her needle, she found plenty to do, for the whole king's household declared they had never seen such beautiful work as hers.

CHAPTER IV.

FERTRAM FALLS UNDER A SPELL, AND IS BETROTHED TO "DARK ISOLDE."

At length the king returned from his long tour accompanied by Fertram, and as soon as the ships were in sight, the queen and her daughter drove down to the shore to welcome them home.

When they were all four seated in the golden chariot on their way back to the palace, both the king and Fertram were greatly surprised not to see fair Isolde, and asked why she had not come down to meet them.

Then the queen, pretending to weep, and putting her handkerchief to her eyes, said that some time after the king's departure, the tower in which Isolde lived had been burned to the ground ; no one could find out how the accident had happened, but they thought the princess must have carelessly left a light near some of the curtains.

This terrible calamity was a fearful blow to Fertram, so, instead of joining in the festivities to celebrate the king's return, he shut himself up in his own rooms, and would see no one for several weeks.

At last the queen herself came to his door, and as she would take no denial, he was at length obliged to open it. When she entered, he saw she held a golden goblet in her hand, filled with wine. At first he would have none of it; but as she continued to press and urge him, if only just to taste it, hoping by so doing to get rid of her, Fertram took the cup and drank a little. But no sooner had he swallowed the first mouthful than he fell into a deep sleep, and lost all consciousness.

When at last he awakened, all remembrance of his love for fair Isolde had vanished.

The queen, seeing the satisfactory effect of her magic draught, lost no time in sounding the praises of her own daughter, until at length, after much persuasion, Fertram consented to marry her, and a day was fixed for the wedding.

Ere this could take place, however, the future bride had, according to the custom of the country, to embroider and make up both her own and the bridegroom's wedding garments.

Now, dark Isolde was not good with her needle; she was very lazy, and much preferred idling about and gossiping in the stables and kennels, to sewing or spinning indoors.

In her perplexity as to what she had better do, for she wanted to marry Fertram, she sauntered across the stable yard to the kitchen, where the old cook was sitting on a stool, shelling peas, and asked her what she would advise her to do.

"THE OLD COOK WAS SITTING ON A STOOL SHELLING PEAS."

"You ought to be ashamed of yourself to be so helpless," answered the cook, crossly, for she had no love for the new queen and her daughter. "It is all very well for a poor old woman like me not to be able to use her needle, for I have always had to work hard for my living, and my hands soon got too rough for sewing much; but for a young princess like you not to be able to embroider her own wedding-dress! Why, such a disgrace will be handed down for generations! But there, as you *are* so stupid, I suppose I must try and help you. Fortunately there is a young girl here, called Näfra Kolla, who sews as beautifully as any princess; you tell her I sent you, and I dare say she will help you."

When dark Isolde heard this she was greatly pleased, and at once ran up to her room and brought down the various pieces of silk and twists of gold and silver thread, and brought them to Näfra Kolla, begging her to make up the garments. This Näfra Kolla promised to do, and her clever busy fingers finished both the bridal garments the evening before the wedding.

CHAPTER V.

THE SPELL IS BROKEN, AND THE WICKED QUEEN'S DESIGNS ARE FRUSTRATED.

THE following morning the sun shone out bright and clear, and every one declared no happier omen could usher in so auspicious a day.

But when the queen went to her daughter's room to waken her, in place of dark Isolde, there lay a hideous dwarf in the bed.

"Oh, Isolde!" cried the queen, wringing her hands, " what can we do? How was it possible that we both forgot that this is the one morning in the year on which you must resume your own form? Oh, this is terrible! We must put off the wedding, and say that you are ill!"

" No, no," croaked the misshapen figure; "if we once let Fertram off, I know he will never marry me."

The queen remained lost in thought for a few minutes. Then she exclaimed—

"I know what we will do! I will get Näfra Kolla, the sewing girl. She is just your height and size. I will dress her as the bride, and under the thickly embroidered veil no one will notice the difference. Then, after the whole party come back from their ride, you will have resumed your own pretty face and figure. You can then change with Näfra Kolla, and none will be any the wiser."

"But will not Näfra Kolla talk about it or object?" asked the dwarf.

"Neither she herself nor any one else will know anything about it," replied the queen. "You leave it all to me."

In a short time the queen went to Näfra Kolla's room, and brought her a hot cup of coffee.

"Drink this," she said; "I am sure you must be wearied out with all the work you have done, and this will be a tiring day for you."

Though Näfra Kolla was not thirsty, she did not like to refuse the queen, thinking she really meant it kindly; but no sooner had she swallowed the coffee than she seemed to fall into a sort of trance. It seemed to her as if she were Isolde again, and that this was her own wedding-day. She was dressed in the bridal garments, and the richly embroidered veil was thrown over her; then, after the wedding ceremony was over, the whole bridal party went for a ride through the forest. It all seemed like a strange dream to the girl.

As they passed the blackened ruins of Isolde's tower, Näfra Kolla murmured—

> "Once thou wert bright and fair,
>   Now thou art burnt, oh chamber mine."

Fertram bent forward on his horse, and asked her what she had said. But she gave him no answer.

Shortly after they came to a big lime tree, whose sweet blossoms scented the whole air, and Näfra Kolla murmured—

> "Behold this giant linden tree
>   Beneath whose shade Fertram and Isolde
>   Plighted their troth forever and ay.
>   And he will hold to it yet!"

After riding some little distance further, they came to the deep trench.

Looking down into it, Näfra Kolla murmured—

> "But for my dear mother's golden gifts,
>   Here would my life have ended."

Once again Fertram asked her what she had said; but still she remained silent.

At last, just as the sun was setting, they returned to the palace. Näfra Kolla dismounted and went up to her own room; but scarcely had she sat down, than a sudden giddiness seized her, all grew dark before her eyes, and she lost consciousness.

Then the queen, who had been waiting for her, came forth from behind a screen where she had been hidden, and, taking off the bridal garments, she hastened with them to dark Isolde's room. The latter had now regained her fair form, and was quickly robed in the rich garments of the bride, after which the queen returned to Näfra Kolla and dressed her in her usual dress.

Presently Fertram came for Isolde, and sitting down beside her, asked her what she had said during the ride, when they passed the ruins of her tower.

" I really cannot remember what I said," replied Isolde.

" But you must tell me," said Fertram.

Then Isolde went to her mother and asked her what Näfra Kolla could have said. So the queen told her, and Isolde returned to Fertram and repeated the words.

But he felt strangely dissatisfied.

" I should also like to know what it was you said when we passed beneath the great lime tree, and when we came to that deep trench in the forest."

" I really cannot recollect all I said," replied dark Isolde, crossly. " I am sure it was nothing of any importance."

" Nay, but I insist upon knowing," said Fertram, " you seemed so strange and not at all like yourself; you must tell me ! "

So Isolde once again went to her mother, and the queen said that when they came to the great linden tree, Näfra Kolla had said—

> "Behold the giant linden tree
> Beneath whose shade Fertram and Isolde
> Plighted their troth forever and ay.
> And he will hold to it yet!"

and that when they arrived at the deep trench, she murmured—

> "But for my dear mother's golden gifts,
> Here would my life have ended."

When dark Isolde returned to Fertram with these answers, she thought, "Surely now, he *must* be satisfied."

But all these replies had just the opposite effect, for the more he heard, the more strange and startling did it all appear to him.

"Oh, my lost fair Isolde," he cried, "would that I could learn the truth of all this!"

Then suddenly it seemed as if a veil were lifted from his memory, he recollected all his love for his cousin fair Isolde, and how different she was in every way to the dark maiden beside him.

"Oh, Isolde, my own fair princess," he cried, "would that I could see you once again and hold you to my heart! But as you are dead, and this is not possible, may I also die, and so be with you!"

Scarcely had these words passed his lips, when a soft light suddenly filled the room, and lo! in the open doorway stood his own fair cousin, more sweet and beautiful than ever.

Stretching out her arms towards him, she said— "Oh, Fertram, your love and faithfulness have conquered and overcome the wicked spells of my stepmother. If you indeed are still true to me, we may yet defeat her, and all will be well!"

"Isolde, my own Isolde," cried Fertram, "can it really be you, or is it only your spirit; and are you not dead, as they solemnly assured me?" And he drew her lovingly towards him.

At this moment, the queen rushed into the room, speedily followed by the king.

When she saw that her wicked scheme had fallen through, she gave a great scream, which shook the whole palace. In an instant she was changed back into the wicked giantess she had originally been, and her daughter, who was behind her, became again the ugly little dwarf.

The king, in his anger at the terrible deception that had been practised on him, wanted then and there to order them to be instantly killed; but, at fair Isolde's petition, they were sent back to their own island, and bound never to quit it on pain of instant death.

Then a fresh, and, this time, a very merry wedding feast was ordered, which was much more magnificent than the last one. The tables were laden

"With peacocks roasted
And peacocks spiced,
With fishes boiled
And fishes fried,
With mimjam and pimjam
And multum salve;
The wine that was drank
Was primat and claret,
As well as the wine of Garganus."

Then all the guests, ere their departure, were laden with presents from the king's treasure-house; and when, after some years, the old king was gathered to his fathers, Fertram and Isolde reigned jointly, and lived long and happily, seeing their children and great-great-grandchildren around them.

PRINCE HLINI.

IN a far country, there once lived a king and a queen. They had an only son, called Hlini, who even as a child showed wonderful talents, and grew up the handsomest, cleverest, and bravest man in all the land.

One day, the prince went out hunting with some of the courtiers. It was a beautiful morning; the sun shone with unusual brilliancy, birds and game of all kinds were plentiful; and, well pleased with their good day's sport, the whole party turned homewards as the afternoon shadows began to lengthen, when suddenly a thick fog arose, which soon completely surrounded them. They lost sight of the prince, and it was only with great difficulty that they made their way back to the castle.

When the king heard that his son had not returned, he became very anxious; and the fog having somewhat lifted, he at once sent out messengers to try and find him. But although they searched in all directions for three days and nights, they

could find no trace of him,—no one had heard of or
seen Prince Hlini.

This sudden disappearance of his son greatly
grieved the king; and when, on the evening of the
third day, the messengers returned without any
news of him, the king retired to his room, and,
throwing himself on his bed, gave way to the deepest grief. In vain the queen tried to cheer him,
telling him that Hlini was so brave and clever, he
would be sure to return safely. The king would
not be consoled, and said he would gladly give the
half of his kingdom to any one who would bring
him back his son.

Now, not far from the palace, in the middle of a
wild moor, covered with yellow gorse and purple
heather, there lived an old man in a little cottage
with his only child, a daughter called Signy, who
was both beautiful and clever. They were very
poor, but lived happily and contented on wild honey
and the berries that grew on the moors. When
Signy heard from the shepherds that the prince had
disappeared and that the king had offered the half
of his kingdom to whoever should find him, she
begged her father to let her go in search of him.
At first he was very unwilling to part with her,
dreading the dangers she might have to encounter;
but Signy said she felt quite sure she would succeed

in her search. All she wanted was a pair of new
shoes and some food. And so, after a little more
persuasion, her father gave her his blessing and
started her on her journey.

Signy wandered on for several days, resting in
the evenings in some sheltered nook, and ever going
towards the north. It was now mid-summer, the
days were long—in fact, there was scarcely any
night; and on the fourth evening, just as the sun, like
a huge red ball, was setting in a bed of crimson and
gold, only to rise again, Signy saw some rocks in
front of her, in one of which was a huge cave.
Listening carefully for a few minutes and hearing
no sound, Signy entered very softly, and there she
saw two beds : one was covered with a beautiful blue
silk quilt, embroidered with gold ; the other had a
crimson velvet quilt, embroidered with silver. Going
cautiously forward, she saw the prince, lying fast
asleep on the bed with the golden quilt.

Signy was delighted with her discovery, and went
up to him to waken him ; but though she shook him,
at first gently and then more roughly, she found
she could not rouse him. Looking up, she saw some
strange letters, or *runes*, cut into the wooden headboard of the bed.

Now, though her father, who was a learned old
man, had taught Signy to read *runes*, she could make

nothing of these.   She therefore determined to wait
and see who the owner of the cave was, and discover-
ing a narrow recess near the opening, she crept
quietly in.

Hardly had she got safely into her hiding-place
than she heard a terrible noise, like a peal of thunder.

"SIGNY ENTERED VERY SOFTLY."

The earth began to quake, and presently two frightful giantesses entered the cave.

As they came in, the taller and elder of the two
cried out angrily, "Pah! I smell the smell of a
human being here!"

"Of course you do," replied her sister, "seeing
that Hlini the king's son is asleep here."

They then went to the bed on which Hlini was

lying, and moving the headboard, on which the *runes* were carved, to one side, out came two beautiful silver swans.

"Sing, my beautiful swans, sing, and waken Hlini," cried the giantesses.

And as the swans obeying, sang a lovely sweet song, the prince awoke.

The young giantess then brought him a silver tray laden with delicious fruit and wine; but the prince would not touch anything.

"Will you marry me now?" then asked the giantess.

"No, no, and again no!" cried the prince.

"Then sing, sing, my beautiful swans, that Hlini may go to sleep again," she called out angrily.

And as the swans raised their voices in a sad, plaintive melody, the prince fell back on the bed, and was soon in his magic sleep again.

The two sisters then lay down on the other couch with the silver-embroidered quilt.

In the morning they again wakened Hlini in the same manner, and offered him food, which, however, he angrily refused; whereupon the younger giantess again asked him if he would marry her; and when he refused, as before, the sisters put him to sleep by the song of the swans, and then left the cave, closing it as they went out.

After waiting a little while to make sure that the wicked sisters were not coming back again, Signy came out of her hiding-place, and moving the headboard of the bed, as she had seen the sisters do, she called to the swans, and as they sang their song, the prince awoke.

He was greatly surprised to see Signy in place of the hideous giant sisters, and thanked her warmly for her help, asking how she had come there.

Then Signy told him how much his father sorrowed at his mysterious disappearance, and that she had determined to try and find him.

Hlini was very grateful, and told Signy that after he had got separated from his friends in the fog, he had suddenly encountered the giant sisters, who, having their swans with them, put him to sleep before he had time to fight them or get away, and that they had then forcibly carried him off to their cave; and that the younger sister, as she had no doubt heard, wanted to marry him. But this he had steadily refused to do. As long as he remained firm, they could only keep him there asleep; but he added he would rather remain thus forever than marry the ogress.

When he had finished his tale, Signy said, " Now the first thing we must do, is to find out the meaning of the *runes* on the headboard. When, therefore, the sisters come in this evening, do not refuse their food (for you will want all your strength to get away), but be friendly with them, and then ask them what the letters mean, and also what they do all day while they are away."

Hlini said he would certainly follow Signy's advice. Then, finding a chessboard and some men on a shelf they sat down and amused themselves playing and chatting, till they thought it was drawing near the time when the giantesses usually returned; then Signy called the swans and put the prince to sleep, as she had seen the sisters do, after which she hid herself in her dark corner.

Soon she heard the sisters returning, and presently they entered the cave.

"I certainly *do* smell the smell of a human being," said the elder sister, sniffing angrily round the cave.

"Nonsense!" replied the younger one, who, having lit the fire, was anxious to get their supper cooked. "Of course you smell it when Hlini is here."

"But this is a different smell," persisted the elder sister; and Signy, seeing her peering about feared she would discover her.

But the younger sister, having plucked and cleaned the birds they had caught, told her elder sister she

must cook them at once, as she was about to waken
Hlini; and, going up to the couch with the gold-
embroidered quilt, on which Hlini was lying asleep
she called forth the swans, and wakened him.

By this time the birds were cooked; and when,
she asked him if he would take any food, instead
of refusing, Hlini said he felt hungry, and would
join them at their supper.

The younger giantess was greatly pleased, and,
after helping him to fruit and wine, asked him
whether he would not now make her his wife.

But Hlini said he must first know more about her
and her sister before he could decide.

" What, for instance, is the meaning of those *runes*
carved on the bedhead ?" he asked.

" Oh," replied the giantess graciously, " the words
are—

> " ' Fly, fly, oh bedstead mine,
> And carry me whither I will.'

You have only to sit down on the bed and repeat
those words, and immediately you are carried to
whatever place you wish to go."

The prince was delighted when he heard this, as
he hoped it would enable him and Signy to escape.

" And what do you and your sister do all day
when you are out ?" he asked.

" Well, we roam about, looking for some man,

woman, or child, for our dinner, for we always prefer them to birds or animals ; and then, when we get tired, we sit down under a tree and play with our 'life egg,'" replied the giantess.

"I suppose you have to be very careful when you are playing with your life egg?" asked the prince.

"Yes, indeed we have to be," answered the giantess, "for if it were broken, we should both die. But there is no fear of that," and she gave a loud laugh, "we are much too careful; it can only be broken by a human being ; and whenever one of them comes near us, we soon catch him and eat him."

The prince now declared that he felt so tired, he really must go to sleep ; and though, before calling the swans, the giantess again asked him to marry her, he said he could say nothing till the morning, so he was put to sleep as before.

The next mornings, after the sisters had wakened him and given him some food, they asked him if he would go to the woods with them ; but Hlini said he still felt very tired, and would prefer to rest, so the sisters put him to sleep again and went away, closing the cave after them.

Waiting a short time, so as to make quite sure that the giantesses would not return, Signy presently came forth from her hiding-place and awakened the prince.

"Get up quickly," she said, "for we will follow the giantesses into the wood. Take with you your hunting spear which stands beside the bed, and when they begin to play at 'throw and catch' with their life ball, you must throw your spear at the egg; but keep a clear eye and a firm hand, for, remember, if you miss, both your life and mine will be forfeited."

"Never fear," said Hlini; "there is too much at stake. I will be careful." Then they seated themselves on the couch, and both repeated the *rune*,

> "Fly fly, oh bedstead mine,
> And carry me whither I will."

And immediately the bed rose up, the wall of the cave opened, and passing swiftly through the air, it landed them amid the leafy branches of a huge oak tree.

Peeping cautiously down, they saw the two giantesses sitting at the foot of the tree; one was holding the golden life egg in her hand, ready to throw it at her sister, and both were laughing loudly, as the egg flew backwards and forwards between them.

Watching his opportunity, Hlini threw his spear just as one sister was poising it in her hand, and as the point of the spear hit the egg, it broke in half.

At the same instant, both giantesses fell back

dead, a stream of dark-colored poison poured from their lips, and huge deadly black and yellow fungi sprang up and speedily covered them completely.

Hlini then seated himself beside Signy on the couch, and immediately they were carried back to the cave.

Here they found, on searching round, an immense quantity of gold, silver, and jewels; and having laden both beds with these and the two silver swans, they each sat down on one, and, repeating the *runes*, were speedily transported to the hut of Signy's father, who was delighted at his daughter's safe return, and made Hlini very welcome.

The next morning Signy went to the king's palace and demanded an audience, and the king, having admitted her, asked her who she was and what she wanted.

"I am the daughter of the old man who lives in the little hut on the moor near your palace," replied Signy, "and I have come to ask what reward you would give me if I bring your son back to you safe and well?"

The king laughed good-naturedly. "I do not think I need trouble to answer that," he said. "There is not much chance of your finding him, when so many others have failed."

"But if I succeed," persisted Signy, "will you

20

give me the same reward as you have promised to others ? "

" Certainly," replied the king; "if you succeed in bringing back my son safe and well, I will not go back from my word."

Then Signy returned to the hut, and begged the prince to return with her to the palace; and together they entered the great audience hall.

When the king beheld his son, whom he had mourned as dead, alive and well, he was greatly rejoiced, and made him sit down on his right hand and relate the story of all that had happened to him since the day he became separated from his friends during the chase.

When Hlini seated himself beside the king, he begged Signy to take the seat on his other hand, and then began the relation of all his adventures— telling of his imprisonment in the cave, and how Signy had freed him, and saved his life by rescuing him from the hands of the wicked giantesses.

When he had finished, he rose from his seat, and, standing before his father, asked his permission to take Signy as his wife. To this the king willingly assented, saying that no reward could be too great for her, who had restored his son to him. So orders were at once issued for the preparation of a magnificent wedding-feast; all the great nobles of the

kingdom were invited, neither were the poor forgotten. There was ample provision made for all,
and every one praised the king for his right royal
hospitality, for each one received rich gifts ere they
returned home. Signy's father was made the king's
librarian, and put in charge of the royal manuscripts ;
and Hlini and Signy lived long and happily together,
surrounded by their children and grandchildren.

FERTRAM AND HILDUR.

LONG, long ago, in a distant land, there lived a
king and queen, who were quite happy, save for
one thing—they had no children. Some years
passed, and then, to their great joy, a little baby
girl arrived, who was named Hildur. When the
christening feast came to an end, the king, who was
devoted to hunting, set out with his courtiers for a
long day in the great forest which surrounded the
castle. Nothing unusual happened until the hunting
party began to turn homewards. The king was
riding alone, a little in front of his gaily dressed
retinue, when he suddenly saw an enormous dragon
flying swiftly through the air towards him, holding
a small child in his talons. In an instant the king
drew his bow; the arrow, shot by his practised
hand, sped to its mark, and the monster fell to the
ground, pierced through the heart. The king leapt
from his horse, and by the time his courtiers reached
his side, he was holding in his arms the rescued child,
a beautiful boy of about a year old, quite unhurt.

There were plenty of willing arms ready to carry
the little fellow; but the king refused.

"I rescued him; and now he shall be a playmate for my little daughter," he said. And the whole party went back to the castle.

Years passed on. The children grew up together, and loved each other dearly. The king and queen had named the little boy Fertram, and they treated him in all respects like their own child. If one of the little ones had a present, the other had the same, and at last they were never happy if they parted even for a day.

Now, Hildur's grandmother was deeply versed in all kinds of magic arts, and even when the young princess was still quite a girl, she taught her many of her secrets. The child was the one being whom she loved. On the other hand, she had an unreasoning dislike to the boy who had so strangely become part of the family, and when she saw the affection of the young people for one another, she determined to poison Fertram.

"Never shall my beloved grandchild wed this foundling boy," she said to herself. "The son of one of our rich neighbors is the mate I destine for her."

So she waited for an opportunity.

One day Fertram came in very hungry from a long day's hunting. The grandmother caused a dainty dish to be set before him, and begged him to partake of it. But Hildur, who had noticed her grandmother's dislike to the young prince, came in at the moment, and, seeing the dish was poisoned, prevented his eating it.

Another time the grandmother attempted to kill him as he lay asleep in his bed, but Hildur again divined her intentions. She warned Fertram, and they placed a log of wood in the bed. When night came, the old woman entered, and with a dagger pierced the figure in the bed, as she thought; but, to her surprise, the weapon remained firmly fixed in the log, whilst her hands were fastened to the handle, and she had to remain thus until morning broke, when the spell gave way.

Twice had Hildur thus been able to save Fertram, but they both saw that he was no longer safe. At any moment the old woman might exercise some magic art, and prevent Hildur saving him again. They decided that they must take some other course.

One morning early, before even the sleepy guards at the gate were awake, the young princess and Fertram passed through, and turned their steps towards the unknown world lying beyond their own grounds. At first they wandered through fields, and found the way easy.

"It was the only way, Fertram," said Hildur, when the young man regretted leaving without a word of thanks or love to those who had cared for him through the long years since his childhood— "it was the only way. Nowhere in my father's castle would you have been safe, and my grandmother would only have vented her anger upon my parents, if they had known of our flight."

At length a small river stopped their way. In an instant Hildur changed herself and Fertram into trout and, glittering in the sunlight, they leaped into the water. Hardly had they got below the surface when they saw the grandmother walking along the bank of the river. She had tracked them at once, and now used her spells to try and catch them in their present form. The day wore on, but her art was useless—nothing would entrap the wary trout; and at last, filled with rage, she retraced her steps to the castle.

It was sunset now, and the two young people, having resumed their natural shape, pursued their way into the forest.

"We must no longer take the form of fish," Hildur said. "Even now grandmother will be weaving a magic net, out of which no fish can possibly escape."

And up in her tower, the grandmother went on, weaving, weaving. At first the work went smoothly; but soon the netting became entangled, the knots no longer held together, and her spells showed her that the fugitives were no longer fish, but had resumed their own forms.

"Go forth immediately," she said to her servants. "Take every one who can be spared. Search all through the forest, and kill every living thing that you see."

So the servants searched all day in every direction, but not a creature was to be seen. At last, as night drew on, they met two beautiful dogs; they were the most magnificent animals they had ever seen. But, although they were quite friendly with the servants, they did not allow themselves to be touched. The men therefore returned to the castle and told what had happened.

The wrath of the grandmother was terrible to see. She knew at once that the dogs were Fertram and Hildur, and she commanded the servants to be thrown into the dungeons for not carrying out her orders.

Hildur, by her magic power, knew what had taken place.

"We must not stay here, Fertram," she said sadly; "my grandmother will never rest now until she kills us. Even her love for me seems to have turned to hatred."

"But what can we do?" Fertram asked. "Better

let me go by myself out into the world, and do you return. Then all will be well."

But Hildur made no answer. Presently she unfolded a square of green cloth.

"Sit on this beside me," she said.

In a moment they were floating high up in the air. The day wore on. Sometimes they were borne along swiftly by a strong breeze, then a soft gentle wind would come and seem almost to rock them to sleep, till just as the sun was setting, and the sky was one blaze of gold and crimson, Hildur made the cloth descend slowly to the earth again, and they found themselves in a great flowery plain. Magnificent trees shaded it here and there. A beautiful river wound its way gently through luxuriant banks covered with ferns, and in the distance rose the tower of a great city, surmounted by a magnificent castle, standing out distinctly against the sky.

"Fertram," Hildur said in a low voice, laying her hand on his arm, "this is your native land. You are the son of the king who once reigned here. Now he has been dead for some years. When you were only a year old, your mother carried you into the beautiful orchard which lies at the foot of the castle, when suddenly a great dragon swooped down, tore you from her arms, and she saw you no more.

Your father grieved even more for you than your mother; you were his only child, and the loss preyed upon him, till at length he died of grief. The kingdom will soon have no ruler, for your mother, who hid her grief for your father's sake, is now pining away, and they fear for her life too. Now, Fertram, you must go to her, tell her your history, and receive the kingdom from her hands."

"Hildur, dear Hildur, can it be true? Have I really a mother of my own, as you have? It is almost too delightful to believe. Come, let us hasten to her!" cried Fertram.

"No," Hildur answered; "I must not go with you. You must go alone. But I will remain quietly in that small hut which is under the great tree yonder, until you come for me. But, oh, Fertram," and she clasped his arm with her two white hands, "remember I am alone in a strange country; do not forget me."

"Forget you, when you have been everything to me all these years! Hildur, how could I? Such a thing could never happen. I love you better than myself."

"Yes, I know," Hildur answered; "but I fear some evil. I know not what."

Then, to prevent her grandmother's spells taking effect, she rubbed some salve out of a small box she carried over his hands and face, and bade him a sorrowful farewell.

Fertram embraced her tenderly, laughed away her fears, and then took his way towards the town. He looked very handsome, as he turned once more to wave his cap to her, and the sun's rays lit up his fair hair. She watched him till she could see him no longer, and then went on to the little hut she had destined for her temporary abode.

Fertram only stopped once on his way to the city. Feeling tired with the long journey, he sat down under an oak tree, on a grassy mound. While he was resting, a beautiful dog came up, and as he patted and stroked it, the dog licked his face and hands. Immediately Fertram forgot all his past life, and that Hildur was waiting for him in the hut under the trees.

Having rested, he rose up and pursued his way into the town.

" Can I see the queen ? " he inquired. " I have news for her, which will give her joy."

At first no one paid any heed, but the youth's noble appearance struck the courtiers, and at length he was admitted into the palace.

There he was brought before the queen, who was lying, pale and languid, on a great couch of rich silks and cloth of gold. When he bowed before her, she rose to a sitting position, startled out of her apathy and weakness by his likeness to the dead king.

"Who is this youth? Where does he come from?" she asked.

"Madam," the courtiers answered, "he is a stranger, who craves admittance as a bearer of good tidings to your majesty."

Then, in a few words, Fertram told his tale. Before it was done he was clasped in the loving arms of his mother, who felt it was indeed her long-lost son. The court was summoned together to hear the glad tidings, the news was proclaimed in the streets of the city, the queen gave the government at once into the hands of her son, and the young king was crowned amid universal rejoicings.

Day after day went by, Fertram was absorbed with the affairs of his kingdom, and his love for his mother. All thought of Hildur had gone like a dream.

One day the city was roused to great excitement by the appearance of a most beautiful maiden. No one knew whence she had come, but all agreed that her loveliness could not be surpassed, and when the queen saw her, she sent for her to the palace, treated her like a daughter, and besought Fertram to marry her. This, however, he steadily refused to do.

After a time, whispers went abroad that the

beautiful girl was not as good as she was lovely. Her fair face was constantly disfigured by an ugly frown if things were not arranged as she liked, and the courtiers began to think that the king was right, after all, in preferring to seek another wife.

Just then one of the royal swineherds happened to lose his way in the forest, and he wandered on until he came to a little hut. There he found an old man and his wife, and with them a fair maiden, whom they called their daughter. Never had the swine-herd seen any one so beautiful, and he determined to stay the night with these people, and if possible carry off the maiden. He found that her name was Hildur ; and when the old people had gone up to bed, while Hildur was closing the windows, and putting things straight before following their example, he suggested that they should go out and look at the beautiful moon rising. But Hildur said—

"I must first make up the fire on the hearth."

The man offered to do it for her ; but no sooner had he knelt down than his hands became fastened to the hearth. In vain he struggled to get away, it was all of no avail. Hildur was nowhere to be seen, and it was not until morning that he felt free once more. Then, rising to his feet, he fled from the uncanny place without once looking back.

When he reached the castle, his fellow-servants soon heard the whole tale, and the report of the beauty of the woodcutter's daughter was circulated from one to the other. The royal huntsman thought he, too, would like to see her. So, setting off at once, he reached the hut, and begged for a night's rest. The old people granted it willingly. The beautiful girl was still there, and the huntsman in his turn planned to carry her off that night. He begged Hildur to come for a walk, as it was such a beautiful night. But she refused.

"My time is too fully occupied for idle wanderings," she said. "Will you help me by locking up the door for the night?"

"Willingly," said the huntsman, intending to put the key in his pocket and carry her off later on.

But no sooner had his hands touched the lock, than they remained fastened to it. A mocking laugh behind him made him look round, and he saw Hildur disappearing up the stairs to her room.

When the sun was well up in the sky, and the old couple beginning to stir, the huntsman found he could remove his hands, and he hurried off shame-faced to his home.

Shortly after this, the king was out hunting in the forest, when suddenly a thick black fog enveloped everything. He lost his way completely, and became separated from his people. At length, after some hours, he arrived at a little hut, knocked joyfully at the door, and on its being opened by an old man, craved leave to rest. He was at once invited to enter; and then the old man, recognizing the king, begged him to excuse the poverty of the place.

The king sat down, wearied with his long wandering, and the old man waited upon him, bringing food and drink of the best he had. Just as the meal was ended Hildur came in, and, the king thought he had never seen any one so beautiful before. She was dressed as a simple peasant, but she looked like a royal princess. The king begged leave to stay the night, as it was still too foggy for him to find his way, and the old man acceded, only apologizing for the poorness of the accommodation.

"I will not disturb you," the king said. "Let me only rest in this room for the night, as I have been doing now."

So it was arranged.

After the old couple had gone to bed, the king begged Hildur to stay and talk with him; but she said she must see to the calves in the stable.

"That I can do for you," he answered; and, rising, he went out into the stable, put the straw and hay right for the calves, and had made everything tidy,

when one of them got out.   After great trouble he
caught hold of it by the tail; but, alas! his hands

"SHE WAS DRESSED AS A SIMPLE PEASANT."

remained fastened to it, and he was found in this
plight by Hildur just before dawn.

   She laughed merrily when she saw him.

"It hardly suits a king, my lord," she said, "to be hanging on to the tail of a calf!"

But Fertram humbly begged her to release him. As she did so, she looked up at him.

"Do you not recognize me?" she said.

"No," replied Fertram, much astonished. "I have never seen you before, I am certain."

"Perhaps, then, I remind you of some one?" she asked again. "Of Hildur, the king's daughter, who brought you back to your kingdom?"

"No," he said again, more puzzled still; "I never even remember hearing the name of Hildur."

Then Hildur went and fetched the little box of ointment, and directly she rubbed it on his hands and face, his past life came back to him. He embraced Hildur again and again, thanking her for all she had done for him, and asking her to forgive his apparent coldness and forgetfulness.

"You, and you alone, have had my love all this time, at any rate," he said; "for I could love no one else. And you alone shall be my queen."

Sitting down together in the early morning sunshine under one of the great forest trees, Hildur told him what he did not know; namely, that the beautiful girl whom his mother had taken into the palace was really her old grandmother. She had followed them, and transformed herself so that Fertram should marry her. Then she meant to kill him and his mother, and seize the kingdom.

"So far I have guarded you from her wicked schemes," Hildur said, laying her hand on his; "but, knowing that the past was no longer in your mind, I have feared each day that she might succeed in winning you. For had you been unfaithful to me I could no longer have done anything for you against her wiles."

Again and again Fertram thanked her; then he bade her a tender farewell, and went straight back to the city. The great council of the kingdom was summoned, and to them the young king disclosed the real history of the wicked grandmother. But she was too cunning to be caught and punished. Divining what had happened, she disappeared amid a cloud of fire and smoke.

Then Fertram, accompanied by a magnificent retinue, with glittering dresses, splendid horses, and all the nobles of the kingdom, went to fetch his bride. She was still in her simple peasant's dress, but her beauty made all forget what she wore. Mounting the beautiful steed brought for her, she rode back beside Fertram to the palace; and on the steps, waiting to receive her, was Fertram's mother. This was indeed a joyful day for her. The wish of her heart was granted, in the loveliness and goodness of her son's bride.

The wedding was celebrated with the utmost pomp and magnificence, and Fertram and Hildur lived happily together, surrounded, as years passed on, by their beautiful children and grandchildren.

THE END.